FIVE STILL MISSING

By

Martyn Tott

To Gary,
A good neighbour
who isn't scared of
Close woods!!

2010

Six Magic Numbers Ltd

cheers,
Mat

oct 2016

FIVE STILL MISSING

Copyright © Martyn Tott

First Published in Great Britain in 2010

By

Six Magic Numbers Ltd

Print Date On Last Page

ISBN 9780956380616

Fiction

This novel is a work of fiction. Any similarity to
persons, places or events is entirely coincidental.

Thanks

Family and friends who took an interest in my first novel and supported me by buying/reading it (or even both in extreme cases), June Whitfield for taking the time to call and endorse it as '*a real page turner*', Jackie Kallen for always having time to encourage me and Katherine King for technical support and help getting my books into a fit state to print.

Special thanks to Laura for her patience, editing, wisdom, support and cooking.

To every reader who buys my books.

Cover Art

Karina Fraser (Silhouette)

Laura Turner (Tunnel)

For more info on books and short films

www.martyntott.co.uk (or .com)

Other books by the same author:
Six Magic Numbers (2009)

Read FREE opening chapters at
www.sixmagicnumbers.info

CHAPTER ONE

I never intended to ruin such a nice guitar by smashing it over a drunk in a tacky bar but looking back it changed everything. Epiphany moments have a habit of happening when you least expect them, it's like hitting your head on a low beam in the pub when you've been concentrating on not spilling the beer in your hand. Sometimes these moments of clarity are good, sometimes they're bad, and sometimes it's a wake up call.

For twenty-five years I'd been running from my past and now I was going to be forced to go back and face up to the mess I'd left behind. We all have our reasons for going down certain paths, the trouble is no matter how far you go or how long you're gone for you take your emotional baggage and pack it in your suitcase.

After travelling the world I had ended up on the coast in Spain, playing 'Miko's Bar' doing my one man set to backing tracks, strumming the guitar as best I could to entertain the holiday drunks. When I had started out playing music I thought that I had the gift, a skinny slick haired rock god straddling the monitors in my tight black jeans. With my dark fringe flailing around, pumping that guitar as hard as I could I thought I was the next Joe Strummer. It was my dream when I set out to conquer the music world to be headlining festivals by now with a long list of 'greatest hits' but reality has a habit of slapping your dreams down hard.

That evening I was enjoying a break, fifteen minutes every two hours. I may as well have been working in a mine because it sure killed me to be doing that but I couldn't afford to have a luxury like pride, I was operating on necessity, basic survival. A little amphetamine helped me get through sometimes but the comedown was hell.

Standing at the bar eating my runny omelette I heard it again, a song called *The Sleeping Gallows* about a highwayman being caught and hung. It was sweeping the world with its catchy chorus, you know those songs that once you hear them they stay with you, like it or not? The thing is this particular tune was familiar to me, not just the catchy melody it was like I knew the tune deep inside. Most of all I soon recognised the artist and I knew where he'd got the title, I'd grown up with him after all and co-written it in a garage in the Close where we lived.

Carl had been my best friend up until I was sixteen. God knows why, he was a selfish manipulating bastard with a crooked sense of humour. Last time I saw him was when I'd punched him out for stealing a girl away from me. He had no right to use that song without my consent. I'd hoped that stealing Charlotte was the last lousy thing he'd do but he was back for more despite the blessing of geography putting plenty of miles between us. One thing I'd learned from my travels was that as time marched on the world was becoming a smaller place. He would have known that it would open up old wounds for me. That was the thing with Carl though, he never thought of anyone else unless they could serve a purpose.

I'd already been asked to play the song long before I'd heard it. You get that a lot in bars, people yelling out song titles when you are halfway through another, they think you should know the entire catalogue of every song ever recorded like a walking iTunes, thinking I could skip tracks like a puppet without a brain. I would usually smile at these people and if I didn't know it say *'I'll learn it for you for next time.'* Of course usually there never was a next time, if there was they wouldn't remember the request anyway because they were so trashed.

There was one lobster-faced drunk that night pushing his luck a bit. He was just another of many who came and went throughout the season to get wired, trashed, knob someone and then go home itching their private parts. However this one was different, a persistent bastard and the straw that broke the camels back or my guitar neck rather. This idiot did the worst thing you can do to a musician he started messing with my guitar as I played while carelessly balancing his pint in his other hand, splashing beer. I pushed him off in between chords and he started edging towards my amplifier and I knew already that if he damaged my VOX then I wouldn't hesitate to boot him off the stage as I had done many times before to similar idiots. One night there had been four of them on stage jumping around and I'd shepherded them off with a deft nudge here and persuasive push there - I have to point out that *stage* meant several beer crates and a sheet of eight by four foot chipboard.

A musician's equipment is out of bounds to everyone except roadies, sound men and the band. And we never, *never* appreciate people coming up asking *'Mind if I have a go mate?'* It's like us saying *'Mind if poke your girlfriend?'*

Keeping the mob in order in a shooters bar on a small holiday island was difficult and these rules didn't mean much to Mr Lobster currently overriding my precious amplifier tubes by turning the knobs up at random. A shrieking feedback cut through the bar and people clapped their hands to their ears.

'Oi mate, no touchy the stuff okay, get yerself another drink.' I shouted, forcing a smile.

He tried to focus on me with eyes like piss holes in the snow going in different directions. Miko, the owner, was looking at me from behind the bar not doing anything about the trouble as usual, he was too penny-pinching to hire a bouncer and told me hecklers were my problem and part of what I was paid for. At the time I was barely covering the cost of the room I rented from him above the club, it was a stinking hole even by my standards and I'd certainly roughed it for years across the globe. The toilets in the bar below my window were so wrecked, most of the seats were torn off or the sinks were kicked in but Miko didn't care as long as they kept buying the cheap booze.

'Come on superstar play the song.' Said Mr Lobster on stage, swaggering towards me again like he was on a lively cross-channel ferry.

'Mate can you just piss right off the stage?'

'Sure.' He grinned and I returned to my riffing. Within a few seconds I felt a tapping on my leg that grew heavier and I looked down to see that the bastard had taken my request literally and was pissing *off* the stage and some of it was spraying on my jeans, the only pair I had.

Mr Lobster then grabbed the microphone from the stand and began screaming down it, the speakers started to feedback again. I nudged him with my shoulder but he pushed me back this time. I kicked out at him and he wobbled back into the amp toppling it off the back of the stage. It went quiet, I knew he'd broken the tubes and they would cost me loads to get replaced.

'You're paying for that you stupid aresehole.' I shouted.

He dropped what was left of his beer on it and turned to have a go at me with his arms swinging. I therefore did what any professional self-respecting bar-musician would do. I hit him as hard as I could with my guitar.

Les Paul guitars are pretty sturdy, you could probably use them as cricket bats but I must have caught him awkwardly as it split in two and flew out of my hands hitting one of the floor length mirrors.

Mr Lobster careered into a group of girls at a tall table, scattering them from their barstools like bowling pins as he went crashing to the floor. His friends stood there waiting to see what he would do but I thought I'd killed him. Then he let out a moan, rolled around, face bloodied trying to find his focus. I was shot through with adrenaline, holding my precious bits of broken guitar the metal truss rod inside the neck dropped out clanging across the floor. He'd just destroyed my livelihood, I was livid but there were about half a dozen of them. To my surprise they suddenly let out a huge cheer, gathered their mate up like a sack of spuds and carried him out of the bar singing the chorus to *The Sleeping Gallows*.

* * *

Miko had to shut the bar early because of the mess and broken glass, he didn't look happy, storming about shouting at the bar staff to get the mops and cleaning gear out. The only time I had sensed any happiness in the bloke was when he was flirting with drunken girls half his age trying to get them back to his room.

I was drying off my amplifier with bar towels when I felt a tap on my shoulder. I turned quickly thinking it could have been Mr Lobster but it was Miko and he had my canvas backpack.

'You're out.'

'Out? That wasn't my fault, you saw it.'

'Here.' He handed me a load of Euros, some of the notes floated down across the stage and I peeled them off the beer soaked wood before they turned to mush. 'We are all settled up now piss off.' He spat.

'Listen.' I said, standing up and following him towards the bar, 'I've put up with a lot over the last six months here, you can't just throw me out.'

'Go.' He pointed to the door.

I grabbed him by his bright coloured shirt and he said something in Spanish loudly. I looked over his shoulder to the door where his arm was still pointing. Two local Police waved at me. They weren't like the Police I'd grown up with, these had guns and I knew it was hopeless for me to argue.

* * *

I wasn't sad to leave Miko's crappy bar and room but it was my home, as squalid and crappy as it was I actually needed at least four walls to call my own. I took my amplifier and stuck it on a makeshift trolley that I'd cobbled together, put the bits of guitar in the case and grabbed my backpack. I ended up down on the beach, looking for a spot to sleep. I'd managed to smuggle a bottle of rum inside the guitar case while I was making my exit so I felt a tiny piece of comfort there.

The night was cool; I wrapped myself up in my jacket and began to sip at the alcohol, looking out to the waves, wondering what I would do next. I'd slept on the beach before but usually with some friends around a campfire, I used to like that as it reminded me of my childhood where we would play in the woods behind the Close. I'd kept the nicer memories and held them in my head as detailed as possible. It hadn't been entirely bad before I'd run away but then again it was so long ago I probably rose tinted it to ease the pain of never being able to go back.

I laid on the sand and stared up at the sky, the same sky I'd seen when I began my adventure across the world over two decades ago. I'd wandered so far from my original path, the one I'd set out on, a rock star enjoying the spoils of stardom. It had briefly gone okay but then I'd slid further and further down until I'd ended up here, alone, freezing my nuts off coming down off cheap speed, drinking stolen rum with just a few Euros in my pocket for company.

In-between the shouts of drunken revellers I began to work out a plan. Sometimes it's best to leave the past where it is but there was a small voice somewhere inside of me telling me it was time, time to take a trip back. It wasn't ideal but I was tired. It felt like I'd been running most of my life and perhaps now was the time to go back and see if I could actually find what I'd been running *from*. They say if you dig up the past you're going to get dirty. I was about to find out if it was true.

CHAPTER TWO

I woke up in a UK Bed and Breakfast, the first time in years. An empty duty free tequila bottle rolled off the duvet and clinked across the floor against a rusty radiator. I felt a sense of dread as my headache arrived along with the realisation that I was only half an hour away from the Close. When you only have a small amount of money in your pocket some people would be excited and relieved to be 'home' but not me. There was too much of the unknown I would have to face if I wanted to resolve some important issues. I had no idea how deep they really were, maybe if I knew what was ahead I would have got the hell out quick but hindsight is a glorious thing we can't touch until we go through the mire to get to it.

I rolled out of the bed and washed my face in the small cracked basin. As I rubbed the rough towel across my unshaven face I thought I saw something in the mirror, a shadow behind me. When I turned around there was nothing except my jacket on the wardrobe door. I always had a vivid imagination but there were times when *he* still actually appeared. It hadn't happened for a while but perhaps being back was stirring up the dead bones of my past more than I'd been prepared for.

* * *

I walked downstairs and nodded to a couple of people who were finishing their breakfast. The landlady, all housecoat and dry foundation rolled her eyes at me. I thought she looked like *Mrs Doubtfire's* evil twin.

'Great. I suppose I need to get the pans back out of soak then?' She said in a rough smokers voice.

I looked at my watch.

'It's not nine o'clock yet.'

She pointed to the one on the wall. It was ten past. I wondered how accurate my fake watch was, it only cost me ten euros on the beach from a bloke who had a basket of them.

'Sit down. You've caught me on a good day.'

'Blimey.' I said as she vanished back into the kitchen. 'I'd hate to see her on a bad day.'

'That's my mum.' Said the man.

'That's a *she*?' I muttered myself.

'I'm sorry?'

'Don't be. You can't pick your parents.' I patted him on the shoulder and decided to help myself to some of the orange juice sat on a plastic tablecloth. It was too risky to try the sticky looking cereals, I watched as a raisin suddenly took off from a bowl of muesli, it was actually a fly and I swatted it away.

The couple stood up and gave me a dirty look. The man was larger than me and I remembered one of my favourite lines from the film *Get Carter;*

'You're a big man but you're in bad shape, with me it's a full time job.' Then Michael Caine clouts the bloke from *Coronation Street.*

I grinned to myself and stared at the guy raising my eyebrow as if to invite further comment if he had a problem but his glare melted away and they left. I'd had my fill of bust ups for the time being, maybe I was really changing at last.

'Good morning to you too.' I said to my reflection in a painting and lifted the orange juice; the jug was stuck to the vinyl cloth and slowly peeled itself free. Whatever happened to hospitality I thought, grabbing the newspaper from the couple's table? I began to read the headlines as I sipped at the sharp tasting juice that must have sat there for a week. It needed some vodka in it to make it bearable but I doubt Mrs Doubtfire's evil twin would oblige me with that.

I felt a rumble in the ground; a familiar train noise running close to the bed and breakfast, calling to my inner being. I had a flashing image of the tunnel a dizzy sensation that made me uneasy. I had to drink more of that rotten orange juice just to snap out of it, the sour taste forcing me to wince and let out a groan.

The newspaper headline I turned to read *'Drunken night at holiday resort ends in tragedy.'*

I closed the paper without reading any more; I had enough to worry about without more depressing news reports. I studied the garish pictures on the wall, wondering how many people had sat there in that room staring at them and what their stories had been passing through this horrible point of rest before going on with their journeys.

'Picture, picture on the wall, open up and tell us all.'

The landlady walked in with a pot of tea. She looked at me then towards the hallway.

'I thought there was someone else you were chatting to.'

'Just admiring your pictures.'

'Oh. well anyway here you are.' The pot of tea slopped about and a splash leapt from the spout hitting my leg. 'You looked like a tea drinker.'

'I prefer coffee actually.' I said, wiping the warm liquid off my dirty jeans. Not that you would have noticed if it had stained.

'Well I've made tea now.' She said, leaning over me and plopping the pot down onto the plastic table cover. A waft of stale sweat and cooking oil entered my nostrils and I gagged.

She wiped her hands down her housecoat. Now she was closer I could see dried egg and grease among the pattern on it. She hovered and I put the paper down and looked up at her, she had the air of a headmistress, someone who hadn't had sex for a long time, up tight and on the warpath with anyone in sight.

'So, what's your business here?' She said.

'I used to live here.'

'What in this house?'

'No in the area.' I said.

'What road?'

'Gallows Close.'

'Never heard of it.'

'Well its a few miles into town.'

'We only came here when the new road was built.'

'The *glorious* new road.' I said.

'I wish we'd stayed where we were.'

'And where is that?' I said.

'Where I grew up.'

I went to ask exactly where that was but decided silence to be a better option and closed my mouth slowly. I wondered if the writers of *The League of Gentlemen* had perhaps stayed there and got ideas from this woman.

'Do you like your bacon well done?' She said.

'Yes.'

'Good job, I can smell it burning.' She turned without so much as a twitch of a smile and waltzed back through the long multi-coloured streamers into the kitchen. A puff of smoke appeared making her look like something out of the talent show *Stars in Their Eyes*.

'Tonight Matthew I'm going to be Mrs Doubtfire's evil twin singing 'You Shook Me All Night Long'.

* * *

I finished the grilled breakfast, the bacon tasted like fried cardboard and the tomato sauce had been distilled more than once with vinegar.

As I went to stand up *The Sleeping Gallows* came on the small radio in the corner. I felt myself cringe at it, I wasn't entirely happy with what Carl had done with the song, it sounded too different compared to the original version I recalled. For the first time I tried to really listen to the lyrics. I didn't remember writing those.

'I love this song.' The Landlady said, appearing like the Shopkeeper from *Mr Ben* beside the table. I turned and watched as she wiped the table free of sauce spots with her apron.

'You didn't finish your egg?'

'No. But the rest was fine.'

'Filled a hole?' she said.

'Yeah just the little Dutch boy.'

She stared blankly at me then looked down at the newspaper. 'Bad news, all of it. Don't know why I buy it, I mean look at this, the lad goes out for a night on holiday and is found half-dead.'

'Yeah it's a pisser. You do take Euro's don't you?' I said.

* * *

I packed up my bag and guitar case. I'd sold my beer soaked amp back in Spain along with what was left of some speed I'd been using to get through those awful nights playing at Mikos'; it would have been a pain in the arse to get shipped over, the amp that is, I wasn't dumb enough to try to smuggle the other stuff. I paid my euro money, persuading

Doubtfire's evil twin that it was fine. She huffed as she held the foreign notes to the light and shook her head slowly then gave me a look like I'd just reversed over her cat, which I probably would have if I'd had a car.

With just a few euros now left to my name I headed out across the main road towards the train station. It was closed and so was the hospital further along. I remembered the hospital well because I'd been rushed there after an accident when I was ten. I often wondered if my problems began that day, the protest that ended up with me in intensive care.

I could remember the room where I'd seen the psychiatrist afterwards. Sometimes I wished I'd visited one later in life, I sure wasn't proud of the scrapes I'd got into and the way I'd dealt with them but I figured I was one of the good guys in the small wars I faced. The thing that really ate away at me was that I'd felt as if I was running all my life but I never really knew what from, for a while I thought it was to forget my childhood ghosts, or to find a better place, to escape the creeps and bullies who I'd scrapped with in bars and wherever I'd had to defend myself but the shadows on my shoulder were always there. How can you pin something like that down and face it if it doesn't show itself?

I decided to squeeze through a break in the fence and head around towards the back of the derelict hospital site. Memories began to return about the happy times, my folks still together back then, Adam still alive. All before things went to hell on a hotdog stand. Despite their seemingly happy marriage my parents had split up the year I left school. They had stayed together for longer so it wouldn't affect my exams but at the time I felt cheated to find out they had been living a charade, probably since I was about eleven, a year after the accident. My dad went to live with my Uncle eventually moving to Canada. It was painfully easy for them to move on and adapt to this new set-up and I never understood why because it did my head in completely.

Mum's new boyfriend was '*Slimy Stu*' as I nicknamed him from day one, he tried hard but you could tell he didn't like me either it was just to keep sweet with mum. He did buy me a Raleigh Grifter bike that was the best thing I'd ever seen until I found out he'd got it on the sly from a bloke in the pub. I was accosted one day in the woods by a lad who said it was *his* bike and he even knew the security number etched under the base of the frame. I didn't know what to say as his dad took it away from me. I ran home to tell Stu but he denied it and wouldn't come with me to try and get it back in fact he didn't even look up from the television, as mum wasn't there he didn't need to pretend he was interested.

I thought I was making it easy for everyone to get out of the picture and leave them to it. My childhood had been pretty good up until then and I wanted to preserve it as best I could. Carl, my supposed best friend had by then betrayed me more than once and I saw no reason to stay around and let my good memories get tarnished. If I ran fast and hard enough for long enough surely I could preserve them. There were also darker things growing in the secret garden in my head. After the accident there were strange occurrences that I couldn't explain, call them ghosts, call them hallucinations, they began to scare the hell out of me more and more and the open road seemed the best place to deal with those.

So I left Gallows Close and for many years it worked. I still kept in touch through postcards and the odd phone call but it always felt like there would be no going back physically. It used to upset Mum, especially at Christmas, she'd always make the invite and I would always have an excuse, I would tell her *'It's triple money playing gigs over the holidays here...'* and then find myself on Christmas day in a crappy bar playing cover songs to a drunken party of strangers then going back to some shitty lodging for a burger, longing for Yorkshire puddings and Mum's crispy roast potatoes. I just wasn't brave enough to go back and face things, not if *he* was there waiting. That's the trouble; Ghosts don't count the days, they can sit tight eternally until they get what they want from you.

Now I had no choice, the two worlds of my past and present were clashing and I was back to referee the match, to see if my fears were genuine and find out what was left in the Close.

The plan was to get in, catch up with Mum and some of the old gang, find Carl and get some credit for the song he'd nicked and get out as fast as possible. Our best-laid plans however can often go to waste and deep down I knew this time *he* wouldn't let me run so easily.

CHAPTER THREE

Nineteen Seventy-Six. I laid on the carpet where it reached the edge of the hardwood floor, the bit I pretended was a moat when playing with my Action Man boat. I was nine years old and the owner of a new portable mono tape recorder. I pressed the red and white buttons together and motioned to everyone in the room to be quiet. The Radio presenter announced the next song and a guitar riff came out of the speakers filling me with excitement and then the drums kicked in and I began tapping my feet on the carpet, waiting for the red needle to flicker in the tiny plastic window.

'Turn that racket down.' Said Dad, peering at me from over his newspaper.

'I'm taping...' I protested, watching as he lowered the newspaper further in a way that I understood to mean 'DO IT!'

Dad was an original Mod in the sixties and had kept his tightly cropped hair in the same style ever since. I'd spent lots of nights going to sleep with the sound of Northern Soul wafting up the stairs. For pocket money I'd polish his loafer shoes. He was meticulous like that everything had its place.

My Uncle James would babysit me and my brother when my parents went out to dances, he liked Elvis and the Beatles and had got me a plastic guitar and lent me his tapes, all delivered on his motorbike. He was a Teddy Boy and had actually introduced my mum to my dad. Uncle James had been out racing his Triumph one evening and after a row at a roundabout had been followed home by a gang of Mods including my dad. When she heard shouting outside my mum had gone out to try and calm things down and ended up whacking my dad with a frying pan. This had caused everyone to crack up and when things calmed down he'd asked her out and that was the start of their romance.

Dad turned the newspaper page again and gave me a stern look. I'd slowly been teasing the volume knob back up.

'I don't care about taping it Davy, turn the bloody thing down.'

'You're ruining it.' I squealed.

The worst thing that could happen was to be recording *live* like that with my tape machine and to have people's voices in the background. When I went to play it back in my room it would be full of annoying things like that and as I couldn't afford to buy the vinyl single back then it was the best I had for entertainment.

'I shouldn't worry Dad, he's not taping it.' Said my brother Adam.

I looked up as he walked past.

'What?'

'You haven't switched the microphone on.'

'Huh?' I did a double take and noticed the red recording level needle wasn't moving. I followed the thin lead from the tape machine along the floor to where the microphone was positioned in its plastic cradle. Sure enough I had forgotten to switch it on.

I kicked at my Action Man tank and it squeaked across the floor bumping into the sideboard.

'Flipping heck.' I said, 'I didn't mean to do that.'

'Hey you mind your bloody language or you'll be straight up them stairs.' Said Dad.

'*You* swear.'

'I'm an adult.'

'I'm ten years old.'

'Nine.' Said Mum.

'Nine and a half.' I snapped back.

'More like nine and a half months.' Said Adam, now working on his Airfix kit at the table.

I pulled a face at him and rolled the microphone lead up.

'Why don't you go upstairs and record yourself singing *Demis Roussos*, he's your favourite isn't he?' He started to sing *Forever and Ever*.

I ran over and kicked him under the table but my bare foot struck the wooden leg hidden beneath the plastic sheet he'd laid out. I yelped and screamed.

'You two, bloody pack it in!' Dad shouted.

I finished rolling about and tried not to give Adam too much satisfaction at watching my pain. I fought any tears rising and looked at my foot, it was stinging like mad.

'I'm going to see Carl.' I said, hobbling to the door and swinging on the handle.

I knew that Carl wouldn't be having the same issues with recording the *Top Forty*. He didn't have an annoying older brother he had a younger sister and the family also had a new stereo system where the tape player was built in, avoiding unwanted interference.

'You're not going anywhere at this time of night and get off the door handles, how many bloody times have I told you?' Said Dad.

'Oh please. I want to see if he taped it.'

'Not in your pyjamas. Let me see your foot.' Said Mum.

I held it out to her and she inspected it.

'Does it hurt when you laugh?' She said.

She started to tickle me. I tried not to laugh, I was still sulking.

'They're not pyjamas they're drapes... like Uncle James had.'

'They're polyester from *Brentford Nylons*.' Said Adam.

'Drapes!' I shouted.

They looked at me in my bright green pyjamas, legs rolled halfway up and top collar pulled up. The trim was in dark blue and in my head they did look vaguely like Teddy boy drapes

'Who do you think you are anyway?' Said Dad.

'Bill 'Ailey?' I said, picking up my plastic guitar and hopping across the room and forgetting about my sore foot.

'It's Hailey, not Ailey'. Look, don't be bloody long.' Said Dad.

'I can go over?'

'Half an hour then you better be back here.'

'Thanks.' I raced into the hall. There was a letter on the mat.

To the Home Owner, 7 Gallows Close.

I went back into the front room, handing it to Dad.

'It was on the mat.' I said, spinning round to leave.

'Half an hour' Mum called out.

* * *

I trotted across the Close towards Carl's house number six, bright green pyjama trousers flapping in the wind. The night was still warm it had been the hottest year since I'd been born and we'd cooled off with washing up bottles and water pistols. Carl's house was so near that we could speak to each other from our front windows, so could some of the other kids in the houses that made up our Gallows Close gang. Carl and I hung out with Loz from number nine and twins Peter and Ian from number two.

All our parents had moved into the new suburban estate roughly the same time in the sixties, coming from the city as newly weds into the suburbs for space, cheaper houses and to start families. Behind the Close were woods that ran for a few miles in both directions. They stretched across to a village church to the North and farmland to the East, Running straight through them and also right under our Close was a railway tunnel, one of the longest in the country.

The original landowner's family had owned the estate since Georgian times and they had refused to let the rail company build an unsightly rail line through it. The train company had no option but to build a tunnel underneath. At several points along the tunnel there were enormous brick chimneys that came up out of the ground and one of them was on the land in between our house and Carl's.

When ancestors had been forced to sell some of the land they refused to let go of one plot right in the middle of where our Close was by one of the tunnel chimneys and so there was a huge gap between our house and Carl's, the land had been fenced off from the Close right back to where the tunnel chimney came out of the ground at the end of the gardens as they met the woods.

We would sometimes climb up and look into the plot; it was overgrown with thistles and at the chimney end we sometimes built a *lean to* camp across the huge roots of a fallen tree. There were lots of rumours about why the plot remained empty some said there were probably ancestors of the landowners buried there. Loz and I reckoned it could be buried treasure and wanted to get a metal detector to look. The truth was actually staring us in the face, the developers couldn't have made it easier if they had tried but sometimes the obvious is the one thing you miss.

Everything seems so much bigger when you are a kid and our world only consisted of a few streets, the woods and our school which we walked a mile to every day.

Hardly any parents drove cars to drop kids off and we enjoyed the walk along a woodland trail past the farm which came out near the School playing fields and the no-go area into the train woods.

Our parents warned us not to go too close to the train tunnel entrance that was deep in the woods behind the farm. In the early days of the railway a group of boys had apparently tried to walk through the tunnel and got caught out by a train. Although there were workmen stations called *cubbyholes* one of the five had been too slow and been dragged into the wheels which made mincemeat of the poor little boy, we were told, mouths agape. My brother Adam told me that his ghost would walk up and down the tunnel trying to find his way home, wailing through the huge brick chimney vents. We could sometimes hear shrieking from the chimney on the empty plot and I believed him. I would open the window and look out, often able to still feel the wind whipping past the window, carrying the echoes of the scream under the slate skies.

I literally looked up to Carl who was a few years older and physically much bigger. He was always getting into trouble but it seemed fun most of the time. My brother Adam was three years older and would never hang out with us although I did tag along sometimes to the park before he spotted me and sent me home. If that happened I would go to his room and play his records on a hi-fi where the lid became the speakers. It had cost Dad fifteen pounds from an Ad in the local paper and Adam was over the moon with it, his pride and joy. I had to be really careful to put every-thing back as it was or he'd give me a dead arm or fart on my head. I hated it when he did that.

I reached Carl's house and knocked at the door, pressing my face against the rippled glass pane in the middle of the wood, watching as a large figure loomed along the hall. I hoped that their mad dog was in the back room. I loved dogs but Bilbo was a lively red setter with a mad glint in his eye and he drooled everywhere. The latch clicked and I looked up to see Carl's dad peering down. Bilbo was by his side, tilting his head to squeeze round and see who it was.

'Hello Uncle Derek, is Carl in?'

'He's in the front room.' He said bending down to pick up a letter like the one I'd found at our house. He pulled Bilbo out the way and I ambled past. The dog went to sniff me and a string of drool went onto my sleeve.

'Ergh.'

'Oh Davy.'

'Yes?'

'You don't have to call me 'Uncle' anymore, just Derek is fine.'

'Dad told me it's polite.' I said.

'Yes but you're a big boy now.'

I shrugged and held my palms up. 'I try to tell my parents that but they think I'm still a kid.'

'Well, you're nine.'

'Nine and a half.' I said proudly.

'Exactly. So just call me Derek?'

I shrugged again. 'Sure.'

'Oh and Davy.'

'Yeah?'

'Why are you wandering around in your pyjamas?'

'They're Teddy Boy drapes!' I said.

Carl's dad had been opening the letter as we talked, nudging Bilbo out the way.

'We got one of those.' I said.

His smile froze as he read the contents inside.

He gave me a funny look.

'Has your dad read it?'

I shook my head and played with the handle of the door into the front room where I could hear music.

'Go through and see Carl, its okay.' Said Derek, smiling at me again, this time it was a lopsided one the kind my teachers would give me sometimes before telling me I'd failed a test.

I opened the door, tripped on a wire Carl had put between some furniture and went sprawling into the sofa arm.

'Argh, me gooleys!' I winced as I folded up in a ball.

Carl was laughing and pointing at me, throwing a selection of toys. It shook the last thought from my mind, the instinctual thought that whatever was in those letters really wasn't 'okay'.

CHAPTER FOUR

Spring Nineteen Seventy-Seven. We'd never been as far as the barbed wire fence before. Sometimes we'd been close but we thought it was electrified and always stayed back. The Farmer knew our parents and we'd get our eggs and potatoes there, but we weren't there to shop for groceries, we were trespassing. We'd walked up the trail behind our houses and then east towards the farmland reaching the boundary fence that we would have to cross to get to the train woods behind. There was a small clearing the other side of the fence where we could easily be spotted but once we made it across there we could run down the bridle path, sheltered by overhanging trees. At the end was the final fence into the tunnel wood; Crazy Rick, an older kid from the neighbourhood had told Carl this route information. He had also told him stories about the ghost boy who had been killed by a train which matched what Adam had told me and if you went into the tunnel far enough you could see him.

We had our wooden guns with us as usual, our dad's had made them for us and we invented our own noises to go with them. Most of the kids were kitted out in their army greens but not me I had my guardsman outfit on. It was always hard to hide in it but I was very proud especially as the funnel shaped Busby hat made me taller than everyone else, including Carl. It just wasn't the best outfit to be playing *War* in the woods in and trying to hide among the bushes in a red tunic didn't help. '*I spy Davy*' was the first thing you would hear within minutes of the game starting.

It had become even more important to reach further into the woods this year now that developers had reapplied for planning permission for a new road. That was what the letters had been about the year before, a link road straight through the middle of the woods. Initially the plan was rebuffed thanks to local support and protesting, but after a period of time they reapplied and got to the next stage. It was a week before the new protests started and Carl said that if we didn't explore deeper into the woods soon then the road could put a stop to it forever.

We crossed through into the bridle path hunching down and crawling in places then we ran down to the woods, Loz, Carl, the Twins and me, in that order. There was a theory that you didn't want to be first in the line or last as you could be either confronted from the front by the *enemy* or picked off from the rear. The order that we would assemble depended on who made the most noise and usually Carl would push and pull his way to second place, the safest position. If we argued then he'd say *'I bagsied it.'* It was easier to let him get his own way, he was a bit bigger than the rest of us plus I didn't want to fight him and get thrown in the stinging nettles.

'You go first.' Carl said, as we stood at the last fence separating the farmland from the train woods.

'I don't know. I need to get back for my tea soon.' Said Ian.

'No you don't.' Said Peter, always the bolder of the twins and older by three minutes.

'Oh come on.' I said, taking a deep breath and leaping over the fence and into the train woods, the place I was not supposed to be. A few feet the other side of the barbed wire felt exhilarating. Loz and the Twins jumped over behind me and we gingerly moved along, slowly walking across the embankment for thirty feet before we could see down towards the edge of the tunnel. To get there you would have to move out from the rugged path and climb down across limestone and thick twisted tree roots.

There was a shout from below. At first we thought it could be workmen but it was crazy Rick. We knelt down and slowly edged ourselves off the top of the path onto the slope and could see him perched on top of the tunnel entrance roof. The surface of the tunnel entrance was made of solid concrete and pointed in the middle like a giant's shed roof, covered in patchy moss, scrawled chalk graffiti and dark stains from years of rain and the old smoky coal engines. The drop below the ledge was about fifty feet onto the rails but Rick was fearlessly dangling his legs over it and yelling like Tarzan.

'I'm the king of the castle.' Rick shouted.

'You're a crazy arse-hole.' Peter said quietly.

'I want to get up there.' Said Carl, sliding down towards the tunnel roof. At either side were tall spiked security railings that ran around the back of the roof area. Bits of rock and chalk rolled down from beneath his feet as he slid towards it.

'There's a bent railing over this side, you don't have to climb out.' Rick said, standing up and aiming his catapult around. He fired off a rock into the tree near us it clunked and bounced off.

Rick was nuts but we were glad he was our friend because he was fearless and a good shot with that thing if *bigguns* came. *Bigguns* were older boys who would come into the woods to smoke or snog with their girlfriends. They might have been bigger than us but Rick's aim was so good that he could get them running as long as he had enough stones.

We'd been caught a few times by these older gangs but they were usually just interested in nicking any sweets or pea shooters and water pistols we had. Sometimes we would fight back if there were more of us and a few times we'd been asked to become *ammo fetchers* for gangs gathering stones as they fought another gang at the opposite side of the ridge.

Carl disappeared behind the railings and then appeared next to Rick on top of the concrete roof of the tunnel entrance waving his arms in the air like *Rocky*.

'Champion. I was the first here.' He stuck a *V* sign over at us as Rick drew rude things in chalk on the roof. The Twins, Loz and me started to edge towards the side of the railings but instead of going towards the gap onto the roof we peered down the drop to our left that descended to the tunnel entrance. I suggested to Loz, Peter and Ian that we beat Carl down to the entrance and they all agreed that this was a great idea. Carl revelled in doing things before anyone else whether it was a wheelie on his Chopper bike, or racing Scalectrix cars, or winning a play fight by making you submit.

'Hey, what are you doing? Carl shouted, spotting us, 'I'm going to be the first down there? I bagsied.'

'Not this time.' I laughed nervously, grabbing onto one of the tree roots that formed a natural ladder down the embankment.

'You're too chicken Davy you wouldn't dare.' He threw a lump of chalk and it hit me on the arm.

'Cut it out Carl.'

'You idiot.' Peter shouted up at him. 'Do that again and I'll throw you down there.'

'Oh I'm scared.' Mocked Carl.

'Why do we still hang around with him?' Peter muttered as he held onto the first tree root and stepped slowly down, the bridge wall to our right side, tree-lined slopes of the embankment on the left. I slid down on my bum in between hand and foot holds with Loz and the twins behind me.

'I don't know about this.' Ian whispered, stopping halfway and bouncing up and down like he needed to pee.

'Get out of my way then.' Said Peter, pushing him aside and moving down.

There was about twenty feet left to descend before I reached the huge entrance, I could smell a rusty metal odour and hear the sound of crackling electricity echoing around a tall grey tower beside the tracks. My heart began to thump more and more in my ten year old chest and I was taking big gulps of air but I was determined to beat Carl for once so I kept going, stopping just at the side of the tunnel entrance and looking back up at the others; they looked down at me but they were terrified, backing away.

'Well come on then?' I shouted, straightening my busby hat.

Ian pointed over my head as I heard the sound of boots on loose gravel. I turned to see a flash of an orange coat, then another, and another as workmen came out of the tunnel entrance on the far side of the tracks, there was barely forty feet between us and to make things worse Carl and Rick were now lobbing stones down on them.

'You, stay right where you are.' One of them shouted.

I span round and ran back to the first tree root, scrambling up the slope, I could hear the men running across the hard rock gravel on the train line. I was much smaller and more nimble in my ascent than the workmen but my arms trembled with adrenaline and fear, my hands slipping on loose rocks as I felt for hand and foot holds. I could hear them getting closer as I reached the top roots; I slipped and winded myself hitting the dirty dusty floor, there was a tug at my foot, a hand gripping the heel of my shoe with a thick workman's glove, I yelled out and kicked free but my shoe came off, the workman sliding back down ten feet and swearing at me.

I picked myself up and got to the next section of slope, running up it as fast as I could, my busby straining on the elastic strap. I must have looked like Billy Whizz from the Beano comic with my legs spinning in the air, climbing the embankment section between the roof and the ridge at the top. When I got to the top I turned left along the thin pathway and tried to leap over the fence, falling over as my socked foot landed on a piece of limestone, I got up and ran through the woods hobbling and feeling the pain of having only one shoe on. From out of nowhere I felt someone on my heels again, there was a hand at my neck, it pinched at my shirt. I turned to see Carl's stupid face. He had an annoying habit when in panic he would sacrifice anyone to escape from trouble and often pulled or pushed people off the path in order to get away himself.

This time it was a shove into a bush and he overtook as I bounced over it and landed in some nettles on the other side. He laughed as he ran away, Rick was behind him and he stopped, lifting me back up and throwing me over his shoulder, running with me down the trail towards the edge of the farmland singing *The Wurzels* in a shaky voice.

'I've got a brand new combine harvester and I'll give you the key!'

We reached the farmers fence near to one of the tunnel chimneys as it began to wail from below, a screaming out into the woodlands, the ghost boy. Sat there on the other side of the fence were the others, laughing and shaking with the after effects of the chase.

'I thought you were going to get caught.' Said Ian.

'They couldn't get up the hill fast enough, I think they turned back at the top.'

I walked over to Carl who was finding it very funny to

see me hobbling.

'One of them got my shoe you idiot.'

'Shouldn't be so slow.' He sneered.

'How am I going to get my shoe back? My Dad's going to go nuts.' It wouldn't have been so bad if it hadn't been my *Clark's Commandos*. My favourites, the shop gave you a metal badge with every pair and they had cost my parents a fortune.

'Thanks for holding me back as well.' I said to Carl.'

'Shouldn't be so slow you wimp I keep telling you.' He threw a fistful of soil at me and I jumped out the way, circling around and I threw myself towards him trying to get a shot with my fist. Carl rolled out the way and slapped me on the head, I grabbed him and managed to get the better of him briefly with a punch on the nose before Peter lifted me off and separated us.

'You're pathetic Carl.' Peter said as I flailed around. 'I don't know why we hang around with you anymore.'

Carl stood up wiping at the blood that was dripping down his face and grinning. 'Because I'm the coolest kid you know, you bunch of losers.' He offered me his hand. 'I was only messing about. Come on, who's coming back then to get Davy's shoe?'

'What, to the tunnel?' Said Loz.

'Yeah.'

'No way, that's it for now, we've got a week left of the holidays to do it and we really do have to be back for tea.' Said Ian.

'You should have been in the girl guides Ian, are you having lashings of ginger beer too?'

I looked at my filthy foot and wondered what I was going to say to my parents. I needn't have worried too much as they had far bigger matters to contend with.

CHAPTER FIVE

Back in the present I wandered around the derelict hospital lost in my thoughts, the awful food from the Bed and Breakfast still grumbling in my stomach. Just like my digestion I had uncomfortable feelings thinking about the accident and aftermath that had followed soon after we'd discovered the train tunnel, glad to survive, lucky, they told me, to be alive but I couldn't help wondering if that was the turning point, when my life began to change for the worse. Up until then I had been a happy kid with nothing more to worry about than the new Action Man figure or staying out on my bike as long as I could before I got called in for tea. The accident changed all that.

When I snapped back out of my daydream an hour had passed, I couldn't keep putting it off and I needed to head to the Close so began walking towards the small town along the new road toward the home where I had once belonged.

There was a tight feeling in the air, calm before a storm that I had missed when I was in hotter climates; I never knew people could long for a miserable wet day. The British seasons were a national obsession and like roast dinners on Sundays it was something I had grown melancholic about when they weren't there.

I had been walking for about fifteen minutes along the new road when it began raining quite heavily. I felt tired and strayed from the path into the road just as a passing car skidded to a halt and sounded its horn. I turned to flick my fingers but stopped when I saw an old Gentleman driving a classic car, something from the thirties, God knows how he'd kept it on the road it looked magnificent.

The chap inside looked at me through the sloshing windscreen wipers but he didn't shake his head or shout, he just stared at me with his pipe hanging down from his mouth and mopped his forehead with a large handkerchief.

Walking towards the vehicle I watched the steam from the bonnet rising into the rain, creating a smoky haze around it. I could hear the radio now from inside, a big band tune blaring. I stood and stared at the driver.

'You need to be in a museum like this car.' I shouted. 'You nearly killed me.'

The engine revved and throbbed like a dog warning someone off, the fogged side window began to wind down, a plume of pipe smoke exhaled from the gap and I squinted through the downpour that was now making it hard to see, the rain was so hard.

'Didn't you see me?'

The man looked past me and before I could speak again I heard a noise in the woods, I turned and saw something running across the path just inside the trees parallel to us. It looked like a big dog, it stopped and looked at me and then began to run again. I stepped back off the road and took a few steps to get a closer look. By the time I turned around the old car was gone, pulled away and vanished in the rain-soaked mist.

I carried on plodding along the side of the road for another mile and could now see the farmers lane, I stopped and looked for the trail which had been cut in two by the big new tarmac road, it was roughly where the accident had taken place, years before the road had been finished.

I felt it again, somebody or something was watching me from the woods over my shoulder. I studied the line of trees beside the road for movement but there wasn't anything other than the odd bird or squirrel.

I walked away from the road, across the verge and took a closer look into the edge of the woods, sheltering under some of the thicker trees from the rain but by that time of year most of the leaves were a soggy mess on the muddied trail. The rumble from underground began to shake my feet and a wailing cry echoed from a nearby train tunnel chimney taking me right back to the day of the protest, the day of the accident. There was something about revisiting that wood, the smell and the closeness of the trees that awoke my senses more than ever.

I looked around and behind one of the trees propped up was a bunch of flowers, they'd rotted away and it was just the stalks left, I knew who had left them there. I saw the chunk of bark still missing from the tree and I was now standing pretty much in the spot where my life changed and I closed my eyes, feeling the rain on my face, remembering more than I cared to recall but powerless to fight it.

* * *

It was late spring Nineteen Seventy-Seven, the time of year when summer was pushing through; the wild plants in the woods were out of control, nettles everywhere. I'd never been to a protest before, the first one had just been adults but now I was ten, I was in double figures so I was allowed to go.

Everyone from the neighbourhood was out in force to stop the developers building the new road through the woods. You could reach the Church at the far north side if you followed the trail for about half a mile from our gardens. The Church was safe from development but a corner of the graveyard was to be renovated as part of the plans for a feeder slip road leading to the new road. I heard my Dad say that it would be impossible for them to be able to move graves but it seemed that developers were capable of moving mountains. In my imagination I was scared that skeletons would soon be walking the woods and chasing us like the film *Jason and the Argonauts*.

We were told that we could stay for the protest as long as we were within a marked area by the Church perimeter wall where it bordered the farmers land. Carl's dog Bilbo was circling us and snarling at anyone he took a dislike to and occasionally chasing a hawk that had decided to observe things from the Church gate.

As a kid Carl used to sit on him and try to ride Bilbo like a horse but one day the mutt had grown fed up and snapped at him. Carl ran and told his dad that it had been unprovoked and he was scared and if his sister hadn't seen it all from her window and told them the truth then they would have put the dog down. It had always bothered me that I knew Carl would have let them rather than admit to lying.

The organisers had let the Police and the press know about the protest I knew their faces, they walked around the Close every week telling us off when we were up to mischief and giving us a clip round the ear for causing trouble. The parents knew who they were and we showed them the banners we'd made. I drew things like animals on there because it wasn't just us not being able to play it was all the wildlife and trees in danger and they didn't have a voice, that's what Mum said.

The afternoon started out well enough with journalists and photographers coming to take pictures and talk to us, we had a big picnic, sharing some food with the officers and some produce the farmer had brought along and as the adults chatted about boring stuff we got to climb trees and enjoy the spring sunshine. My Uncle had also turned up with another new girlfriend and a new cassette tape of Elvis for me.

We had no idea of the people who were heading towards the protest. The only indication that our childhood bubble was about to go to war with reality was Bilbo who kept barking and scratching at one of the tombstones in the corner of the Churchyard. Carl's dad was trying to pull him away but he was getting wilder, circling it and whining, howling like a wolf.

My Granddad used to tell us stories of bombing raids when he was a Fireman in the city during the Second World War. Before they happened he always felt calm, like the world had been switched into slow motion for a little bit, the air hung in suspension then all hell would break loose. That's the way I felt as I watched Carl's dad with Bilbo the moment he got the dog to calm down I breathed a sigh of relief before I saw the first of the strangers appear.

They had arrived in a big van that was painted with slogans. I had never seen them before and neither had the police or adults. They instantly tried to anger the Police shouting *'We don't let the man push us around,'* knocking one of their helmets off. Being a kid I didn't know which *man* they meant, I just knew they really didn't like him and they didn't like the Police either.

One of them walked up to us and told us to spit at the Police because they were the enemy working for this *man*. I told him that I'd get a clip round the ear and ran away to find Adam but the arguments began, it got heated and there was too much shouting to make any sense, it made my head spin. Even for braver kids like us who went to train tunnels there was a feeling in the air and it was making my dad act strangely. He was trying to talk to some of these people but they wouldn't listen, pushing and yelling and using words that made Derek tell them to watch their mouths as there were kids about and when that didn't work he punched one of them and Bilbo bit him.

I was starting to feel scared, I wanted everyone to slow down, to stop hurting each other, I'd never seen anything like it before.

Most of the kids got ushered off towards the woodland trail that led back to our gardens but I got caught behind the Church wall, too scared to move. Horses appeared with more police, it was too much information for my little head, a firework flew over and the horses went mad, there was a crashing sound over the back of the Church, people fighting and breaking up the fences for weapons, more arriving from nowhere. I poked my head up and saw my dad as he threw one of the strangers to the ground; he caught sight of me and shouted at Adam to grab me.

We ran as fast as we could across the gravel path into the trail I saw the twins and Loz ahead of us, his *Top Trump* cards spilling on the floor. He was trying to pick them up but it was no use, too many people and horses charging around. I looked down and felt my legs go to jelly again, seeing one of the cards *'Fastest Speed 120mph'.*

We got a fair way down the trail into the woods, about halfway home and started to slow down.

'Follow Loz. I'm going back to help Dad.' Said Adam.

'I'm scared.' I said.

For the first time ever I didn't want him to go away, I wanted us to stay together.

'Look just go home titch I'll be okay.' He patted me on the shoulder.

'Who are those men Adam?'

'Dad said the developers paid them to cause trouble.'

'Why?'

'I don't know. I want to help though. Please just follow Loz.'

He reached into his shirt pocket and pulled out a small model Spitfire plane he had finished painting that morning. I knew it was one of his favourites already.

'Look after this for me?'

I nodded and for a second I thought he was going to hug me. It was as if he knew things were about to change.

Over his shoulder I could see figures approaching. First it was Carl who came flying down the trail yelling, pursued by a wild horse. Some of the animals had been let out of the farmer's stables by the troublemakers and were going berserk. The trail was only wide enough for two people and Carl didn't look like he was going to stop, reaching us before we could even react to what was happening.

Carl blundered into Adam knocking him out the way and pushing me towards a tree then he carried on running. The horse was right in front of us now, Adam was getting up he could see the animal was headed straight toward me. That was when he threw himself in-between the horse and me.

I remember Adam's body hitting mine as the animal tried to jump over us, the wind whipped past as I looked up at it's belly, time slowed down and the breath was pumped out of my body and then my head thumped against a tree. I slumped down to the floor, trying to breathe but no air came to my lungs, my head hurt so much I felt like laughing and I could see brown string streaming everywhere, floating around and landing on me, I later found out it was my new Elvis cassette spooling like streamers at a street party.

I had no air to scream with, to call out for my dad, no time to do anything but slip away into the darkness, into the deep that drowned out the shouting voices and stampeding horses.

CHAPTER SIX

When I awoke after the accident I didn't recognise the voice calling my name. The last thing I could recall was being hit by the horse. I could still smell the dirt and I was in the woods but to my surprise I wasn't hurting anywhere despite my fall.

'Davy. Can you hear me Lad?'

I opened my eyes wider and focussed on the face peering down at me unshaven, dirty and his teeth were crooked. I was scared at first and looked around for my dad.

'What happened?'

'You're going to be fine.'

'We were hit by a horse.'

'Yes, you got in the way but you survived.'

'Where's Adam?'

The man stood up on the trail and grabbed a tree branch bent it and then let go.

'See that? If we don't learn to bend Davy then we'll break.'

'Where's my brother?'

He grabbed a stick, snapping it like a strong man at a circus.

'See what I mean?'

'Why won't you tell me about Adam? I want to see him.'

'You know, a horse won't deliberately hurt you. It was frightened and probably tried to jump right over you but sometimes there's only seconds between life and ...' I waited for him to finish; he seemed distracted, looking around. '... and you my friend are very much alive.'

'Where's my dad?'

'He's fine. It's okay, you had quite a bump there.'

I sat up and looked around. It was dark and we were the only people there.

'Where is everyone?'

'They're all fine.

'But who are you, are you *the man*?'

He gave me a broad smile and a bow.

'Kane Balfour at your service.'

'Are you a Doctor?'

He offered me his arm and as I reached up he picked me up and stood me to my feet. I felt no pain or bruising. I looked at his clothes, in the gloom I could see he had a long thick coat on and knee high folded boots, as he stood to his full giant stature he put on his hat, a triangular shaped one I'd seen in books that my dad read to me from the Georgian times.

My eyes adjusted and I wondered if I was dreaming, I didn't care though because it was better than the last thing I could remember which was being very scared and hitting my head.

'No pain?' He smiled.

'No.' I said, checking for bumps around my body. I felt fine.

'Come, we have an important appointment.'

He untied a horse from a nearby tree.

'I don't think horses like me.' I said.

'Oh come now, there's an old adage, if you fall from your horse then the first thing you do is...'

'Get back on... I remember my Dad told me that when I fell off my bike.'

I stopped for a moment as he held the horse's reigns and walked over to me.

'He also told me not to talk to strangers.'

'But how would a stranger know your name and that you live in Gallows Close?'

He smiled at me and for a moment I saw something familiar

in the eyes.

'I guess.'

With a quick punt of my foot he threw me up and onto the horse.

We rode up through the wood on the trail and I felt safe, secure despite everything, all the anxieties I'd been having before the accident had gone. We went up to the Church where the protest had been, it looked pretty much as it had done earlier that day. We got down, tied the horse and walked into the Churchyard. I got a better glimpse of his attire.

'Why are you dressed funny?'

'Me? Well how do you expect a highwayman to dress?'

'A highwayman like Dick Turpin?'

'Oh always Dick Turpin' He rolled his eyes at me. 'He's not all that you know he's done some pretty sick things I can tell you.' Kane laughed in a heavy loud roar. 'Well maybe another time.'

'You rob people too?'

'We relieve people of things they don't need. Too much stuff can corrupt and spoil, we just re-distribute it at times as a free service to the gentry.'

'Like Robin Hood?'

'No like *me*. Stop trying to compare me with someone in a book for goodness sake.'

I heard footsteps on the gravel lane, three men approaching with lanterns.

'Who's that?'

'My acquaintances Davy I need you to be brave okay.'

'Why?'

'I have to show you something and you mustn't be afraid.'

I nodded as the men walked into the graveyard, they had an exchange of words with Kane and they glanced down at me more than once and then led me to a recent grave, the earth still unsettled, not yet sunken.

'You're not going to bury me are you?' I said.

'No, Davy I need to show you something so pay attention.'

The two at the back with spades and began to dig.

'Don't be alarmed Davy, you are witnessing a phenomenon of our time.' Kane whispered as we watched.

'What are they doing?'

'Body snatchers.'

'Why would you want a dead body?'

'I don't want it but the Quacks, Doctors; they pay good money to research medicine. Especially fresh ones, I mean they're helping science right?'

'Aren't they all rotten?'

'Not this one. Fresh in the ground today.'

I found myself at the side of the grave, watching them and staring into the pit as the heavens opened and the rain fell lightly at first then harder, like bullets from a gun thudding into the ground around us. Down inside the grave I could see thick worms writhing around, the type my dad would love to find in the garden and take fishing.

The coffin was being lifted higher, up towards us and then they gave a big heave as it was tilted onto the edge of the grave, it gave a creak as they put it down, the wooden top was still shiny, like new.

I watched as one of the men banged a metal bar into the edge of the wood, yanked it and then the coffin lid cracked and fell away, a pale white hand lolling out behind it, which made me jump. I stepped back.

'Go on Davy boy.' Said Kane. He pushed me towards the open coffin as the men tipped the body out onto a tarpaulin canvas sheet. I looked down and saw the twisted shape in the moonlight, getting closer I knelt slowly and thought I recognised the shirt that covered the torso. The head of the body was dirty, the hair matted with mud. I leant down and saw the face and it was then that I realised it wasn't covered in dirt, it was blood. I remembered why I knew the shirt and also the broken up Airfix model in one of the limp hands.

'No, that's not him.' I cried, kicking at the dirt to get away. I bashed my knee as I stumbled and looked to see *Five Still Missing* in big limestone letters chalked onto one of the tombstones next to where they had been digging.

I ran. Kane shouted something after me but I couldn't hear him I was into the woods and tearing down the trail, trying to get to safety, back to my house, away from there, from the nightmare. I just had to get back home and check Adam's room, because that was where he *really* was, probably playing with his next model kit.

CHAPTER SEVEN

Walking past the scene of the accident after thirty years made no difference, it was still so vivid, my stomach shifted again, this time it wasn't the food it was a scooped out feeling that I used to get whenever I was feeling intense fear. Sometimes I would pass out when that happened and so I walked away quickly, taking the long way around past the bus stop into the entrance to Gallows Close. The rain had drenched me through, and my hair was plastered across my forehead like I'd had an accident with a tube of gel. My trousers clung to my legs and I knew that I stank I hadn't washed properly for days, the shower in the bed and breakfast had been caked in mould so I'd taken a pass on that one.

Before I could get my sense of the familiar I noticed it, a building that hadn't been there in the Close when I left, there had *definitely* never been anything there for centuries but there was now. A house where the gap had once been between my old house and Carls.

The developers had finally got the plot from the landowners somehow. To make things more confusing in the driveway I saw the gold coloured vintage car that had nearly run me over. I had a closer look, it was a *Crossley*, I remembered that I'd had a model of a similar one from my Uncle when I was a kid, passed down from my Grandfather who had died when I was a baby. This was the other Grandparent, not the fireman. Apparently he'd doted on me and told my parents, *'You need to take this boy to Buckingham Palace, show him to the Queen.'*

When I was old enough Uncle James had given me the car. *'He wanted me to keep it for you especially.'*

It was one of half a dozen that I kept on my window ledge

and would play with when I went to bed, sneaking a torch out and making a garage from an old shoe box.

I could smell old pipe tobacco lingered around the steaming bonnet of the real life version as I walked past, looking for signs of life in the windows. I thought that I could see a shadow cross the upstairs front bedroom, the swish of a curtain, it was difficult in the rain to make it out for sure.

I felt like a ghost stepping in my own footsteps as I reached our old black iron gate. It still needed a pull upwards and as I lifted it I could see myself as a kid on the pathway, waiting for dad to come home from work bringing copies of *Warlord* and *The Beano* for Adam and me until the accident happened, then it was just my Beano.

I was so caught up in my own world that I didn't notice the old man who had opened the front door. He was smoking a pipe and tipping a Zippo lighter into the end, tugging away to keep it going.

'Come on in before it starts raining again.'

'You?' I said, recognising him as the car driver.

My mum appeared behind him and slowly stepped onto the wet doorstep.

'My God, I thought I was seeing things.'
I walked towards her and after an awkward pause I threw my arms around her for the first time in twenty-five years.

* * *

'Dead?'

'You never liked him anyway Davy, you never asked after him once.'

'But I didn't want him dead!'

Stuart, Mum's boyfriend when I left the Close, had died

three years ago in a car crash and she had never told me even though we had exchanged postcards and phone calls every six months or so.

'I'll make the tea.' My mum shuffled out of the door, she looked so tiny not like the woman I remembered but what did I expect after decades of distance between us?

'She'll be okay in a bit Davy, it's quite a shock you turning up.' Said the old boy I now knew to be 'Horace' pacing around in front of the fireplace like a police detective. He had a lived in face and small eyes that weren't afraid to linger when they caught your gaze.

He got his pipe out and tapped it on the shelf.

'Strange for you to turn up now. You could have visited long before.'

'What's it got to do with you Poirot?'

'Nothing at all but I see what it's done to your mother.'

'It's a long story, Ill tell you all about it one day.' I said.

'Not a nice business though is it? When I was living in Madagascar the same thing happened to me.'

'Sorry?'

'I lived out there for years. My father became a missionary after my mother ran off with the milkman, it's a cliché I know but that's why they are clichés they are very true don't you think?'

I looked at him and couldn't think of a thing to say.

'As long as she's happy I suppose it doesn't matter who she's with.'

'I'm not her fancy man.' He laughed, breaking into a cough.

'I don't care, like I said, it doesn't matter to me.'

'On the contrary it matters every bit I can see that you are concerned which would indicate you do care deep down.'

'Listen Inspector, this is my house and my mum. Spare

me the grilling will you?'

He puffed on his pipe and seemed overjoyed that he'd got some smoke running through the tubes at last.

'There is something you could answer though.'

'Yes?' He said, raising an eyebrow like an over- rehearsed am-dram performer.

'How the hell did you get planning permission to build on the plot next door?'

He put one arm behind his back, taking centre stage.

'My Ancestors have always been on this land. Generations of them.'

'Your family own it?'

'No that's not what I said, I said they *have always been on this land.*'

'So tell me what was on that plot, why wasn't there anything there for so many centuries?'

'All these questions, we've only just met.'

'Well you seem to have enough advice for me and you don't know me.'

Horace lit his pipe again; he blew a plume of smoke towards me and gave a self-satisfied smile.

'You know I spend more time lighting and fiddling with this damn thing than smoking it but it keeps me amused.'

'Yeah, I bet it beats the Comedy Channel any day.'

'I'll take my leave now, let you catch up with your mother.'

He left the room and walked out back into the drizzly rain I watched him from the window as he sauntered down the path and turned towards the new house, clouds of pipe smoke billowing out like a small steam engine.

Mum came in with a tray of tea and sandwiches.

'Why are you here Davy?' She said.

'I wanted to see you.'

'Really? It's been at least eight years since the last time

you bothered to pay a visit and even then I had to take the train to bring some documents so you could renew your passport.'

'Mum, it's not like that this time.'

'Davy it's *always* been like that, ever since the accident.'

'Okay, I'm not the best son in the world but I *am* glad to be here.'

I took a sip of the tea it always tasted good there, I remembered the bone china cups with blood red roses on the side.

'There's more than you're telling me.' She said.

'I heard this song on the radio over in Spain it was one that Carl and me wrote years ago. He must be making a fortune out of it.'

'So you came back to get your share?' Mum said.

I walked over and knelt down beside her.

'I came back because I'm sick of running away. I finally felt ready to come back and face up to things.'

She looked like she was going to cry but Mum was forged by years of loss and she blinked it away, rubbing her hands on the arm of the chair.

'You can stay in your old room. It's pretty much how you left it.'

'Thanks Mum, I really *am* glad to see you.'

She rolled her eyes and shook her head.

'So what else are you going to be up to?'

I noticed a picture on the fireplace, a picnic by the coast, Adam on a rock and me holding Mum's hand.

'I fancy taking a trip down memory lane, I came back past the new road. I saw the flowers.'

'I need to put some fresh ones up there, it would have been his birthday next month.'

'Poor bastard.'

'Watch your language.'

'But it makes me so mad.'

'It was an accident Davy.'

'It was *Carl*.'

'Davy, please, you know deep down it wasn't on purpose, there's no rhyme or reason we just have to accept it as best we can.'

I reached over and held her hand, wishing that I could be so forgiving. 'He was always taking things from me and I never understood why. We were supposed to be friends.'

Mum pulled her hand away and looked at a picture on the wall, Adam and I in our football kits with Dad knelt between us at a local Fathers and Sons competition.

'You kept that one up. Didn't Stu mind?'

'He was fine about it, you can't change the past and it's a good photo.'

'Imagine if we could go back to the moment you took that picture, would you do it?'

'Oh Davy, the times I've gone over it but it's better to leave it where it is and concentrate on the future. At least you can actually change that.'

'I'm going to be doing some digging before I can move on Mum. That's why I came back, to sort it out once and for all.'

'The past has gone Davy. Leave it alone.'

She walked out of the room taking the tray and leaving me staring out of the rain soaked window across the Close. I saw someone out there, a small boy circled the pavement on his bike in the rain. I walked to the window and watched him pause outside Horace's house, look towards it then cycle off quickly again.

CHAPTER EIGHT

I took my guitar case up the stairs into my old room. Sure enough it was just as I'd left it. So much for the lecture on moving on. I always thought they'd have turned it into a guest room or something but then again most of their friends lived quite local and Aunty Bea had to kip on the sofa bed downstairs as she couldn't walk far and had to arrive by bus once a year. I knew all this from letters, I'd sent postcards and kept in touch by mail and the phone now and then. It hadn't been enough.

I looked around at the Blondie Poster, my old hi-fi system, with its twin tape decks where I'd make endless mix tapes for Charlotte, my first crush and the girl Carl had stolen away from me. I felt under the bed for my old skateboard with its Kryptonics. It was still there, the bright green and red wheels now dulled with time. I remembered Adam had 'bones' wheels with skulls on them and we would race around with the others in the close especially one Christmas in the late seventies when we'd all got them.

I plugged in the stereo, located a box of old tapes and reached over to the hi-fi, pressed play and there they were, memories and emotions I had blocked out. When you're running away you don't want to keep looking back or you'll trip yourself up and never get away but there is always a tidal wave of memories waiting for you when you finally pause.

I showered and changed into my only other shirt, there were some shorts that were in a drawer and they just about fitted me so I used them while my old rain soaked faithful Levi jeans dried on the radiator. I rummaged through some old school reports and football trophies in a box I'd found.

Underneath them were my medical records, I recognised the scrawl of the psychiatrist on the final discharge papers. I had been in quite a mess from the accident, a ruptured spleen, broken collarbone, fractured arm and ten stitches across my head that luckily were hidden by my hair when it grew back. It had been touch and go for a while and I was in a coma for a whole week. I couldn't work out how I'd been able to go up to the Graveyard with Kane in that state but when he found me I was okay, I was free from pain.

Apart from meeting him I wasn't sure what else was going on when I woke up in the hospital, looking up at my mother crying I could feel the plastic tube cutting my mouth and tried to pull it out, wheezing and gasping for breath. I tried to tell them about Kane and the body snatchers and my nightmare about Adam but they just kept telling me to rest. Shock can send people crazy; take them into new alternate worlds, away from the pain away from the impact of what they are going through and denial was another aspect that's what they told me all those years ago. They also postponed telling me why Adam wasn't coming home from the hospital with me.

I wasn't sure myself why I'd had the vision or experience with Kane. My father decided to try and put a stop to it and he took me up to look at the graves. The further you went back in the Churchyard the older the graves and now and then a grand tomb or statue rose up from the long grass. I had known that Adam would be buried in the spot where Kane had taken me before I even knew he was dead and when I was asked what I wanted to put in his coffin I placed his last Airfix model and my favourite toy car, the Crossley.

Dad and I searched for ages and couldn't find a grave for Kane Balfour, but towards the Georgian era stones there was one cracked tombstone, the one Bilbo had been barking at the day of the protest with chiselled writing so worn we couldn't read it. The side of the tomb had fallen in and I was convinced that was it, that was where Kane had escaped from and come to show me what had happened to my brother. He had written something on it but I couldn't recall what it was.

I had therapy sessions, regularly. At first I had told them everything but the more I laid it out for them the more sessions I had to attend. The psychiatrist would look at me with a sense of self-pity and concern as I repeated myself.

'I keep telling you his name is Kane Balfour a highwayman, he was buried up at the Churchyard. The faded tomb is his I know it.'

'Davy you had a nasty bump and it has, how can I put it, re-wired part of your brain.'

'I would have got away if it wasn't for Carl, and Adam would still be here.'

'I'm sure he didn't mean it.' Said Dad.

'He's always doing it when we...' I stopped short of telling them about the tunnel. That would have got me into more trouble. 'But Kane was so real how did he know me or where Adam would be buried?'

The psychiatrist paced around me, tilting his head and drawing breath.

'I understand your father had been reading you Robert Louis Stevenson of late?'

'Kidnapped?' I looked over at my dad who was nodding.

'Davy, when we get a terrifying experience the brain can sometimes take us places to protect us. It's a coping mechanism or safety valve, you know like on your bike, if you pump it too hard the air comes back up the pump. Well, in the novel 'Kidnapped', there's a fictional character called

'Davy Balfour' who lived during a time full of highwaymen.'

'It's called the Georgian era.' I said. 'I do history at school.'

'And did you enjoy this book?'

'Yes it's my favourite.'

'Right, well I think you probably created this Kane character in your head as a protector.'

I looked at him and then across the room to my parents who were nodding and smiling. They didn't believe me either but I knew what I had seen. I huffed and frowned and the Doctor showed me out of the room handing me a lollipop like I was some sort of kid, which of course I was and the lolly was actually nice but I wasn't letting on.

In the end I decided to stop being so insistent in order to get away from the therapy and was allowed to return to school where I was treated like a hero with the grazes, stitches and scars. I became interested in history and searched the small library at the junior school for more information about the history of the town, highwaymen and for Kane Balfour. I had always been confused that a highwayman like Kane would have such a grand tomb, if he had been caught and hung then he would barely have had a paupers grave. Maybe he had escaped trial all his life. Perhaps I would ask him, I thought. When he appeared again.

* * *

I switched off my hi-fi and went downstairs, Mum had made me ham and eggs to eat, an old favourite that never tasted the same as it did in that kitchen no matter where I ordered it around the world. We sat and ate and drank and tried to fill in some of the gaps between the years. Somehow it could have been days since I had watched my mum sitting there shaking her head about my escapades.

Exhausted from the last forty-eight hours I eventually began to doze off so I headed back up to bed, stopping outside Adam's old bedroom. I pushed the door, remembering as kids how it was risking a dead arm or fart on the head to be caught going in there by my brother.

Inside I could see that just like my room it was still untouched but from a much earlier year than when I had left the house. I hadn't ever really discussed his death with my folks. It was the bedroom of a thirteen year old in the seventies, a Scalectrix laid out on the floor, Airfix models hanging from the ceiling on cotton and posters of the bands he loved, Iggy Pop, The Ramones and The Sex Pistols which my parents tried to ban him from playing so he had to wear earphones. It was Adam who had told me to join a band when I got older because *'It got you the girls.'*

I walked back into my room and looked out of the window at the houses in the Close. I could see some of the lights on in different homes and rooms. The twin's parents were still at the end and I could see a new garage room conversion at Loz's house. The light was on and Mum said he still lived there so I decided that I'd go and see him in the morning.

I lay in bed watching the rain outside drumming against the window and traced a few drops as they fell down, something I used to spend hours doing when I couldn't go out to play. I closed the curtains and looked on the top of the wardrobe, rummaging about for my old photo album. I flicked through it, laughing at the old faces, parties, the Silver Jubilee when the whole Close had been there.

In the back behind another picture where my parents wouldn't find it was a Polaroid, the gang by the tunnel taken in summer of Seventy-Seven. I remembered the day we took it because it was the day we actually did it, the day we went into the tunnel.

CHAPTER NINE

Late Summer Nineteen Seventy-Seven. Being at that entrance to the tunnel was like looking into an abyss. Standing on one of the rail tracks purveying it from the front for the first time right up to the apex of the pointed roof where crazy Rick would always sit. Either side of the entrance were two horizontal brick shoulders stretching out into the earth. There were grey rusted towers with thick cables running above the tracks. Rick said that someone had fallen on them once and turned to ash instantly. I wasn't sure if it was true but I had no intention of finding out and stayed away from them as they buzzed and clicked.

The smell was overwhelming, cold metal after-burn from huge electric currents and locomotives. Thick sharp gravel rocks crunched and moved under our little feet as we peered inside the tunnel, it was even bigger than we imagined.

'I was in the tunnel first.' Carl shouted for the hundredth time.

'First to get run down then we hope.' Peter whispered to Ian and me.

The first cubbyhole was on the right and supposed to be used for workmen and not kids fart arsing around risking their necks. I hopped from foot to foot nervously looking into the darkness. Loz and the twins were hanging around the opening.

'Do you think the wailing ghost boy's body is still here?'

'It's just a story to stop us coming here.' Said Peter.

'Did the monster get him?'

'Davy, there's no monster you wimp.' Shouted Carl from inside.

I could hardly see him but the voice echoed.

'Shut up... there *are* monsters in these woods, I saw it on telly.'

'Monsters and Highwayman?'

'Shut up Carl.' I stepped in further.

'My Mum told me that you were going to be locked up.'

'Shut up for God's sake.' Peter said.

'They're coming to take me away, away, away.' Carl sang.

He had behaved strangely about the accident apologising in front of the adults when I first got home from hospital, he said there was nothing else he could have done to get away from the horse. When the adults weren't around he would tell the other kids that it was Adam's own fault. I challenged him about it several times but he would change the subject as if it had never happened. For months I didn't want to hang around with him but my parents had insisted that life went on and we all lived so close so it was best to try and get along. He may have been evasive about Adam but it didn't stop him teasing me about my therapy.

'Watch the tracks.' Said Loz. 'If you touch both sides you get electrocuted!'

'Oh great.' Said Ian. 'We're all going to die.'

I peered down into the tunnel, my eyes adjusting to the darkness. In the distance there was a tiny arch shaped light, the other end of this incredibly long brick structure.

Carl had picked up some chalk and was writing his name on the walls that ran up close to the track, there was no platform to jump onto and it felt like you would be squashed very easily if a train came through. I could hear a tiny crackle from one of the tracks nearest to where I was standing.

'What's that?' I said.

We looked down to where the tiny arch of light had been in the distance, it had partially disappeared then there was a high pitch whine on the track and when I looked up I could see a light moving towards us.

'It's the monster.' I screamed.

'It's a *train* you twit!' Said Rick who had climbed down off the roof to join us. 'Get in the cubbyhole'

I was frozen to the spot. Carl, Loz and Rick made the first one and the twins made for the next one opposite.

'Move Davy.'

I felt Peter grab me and run with me until we jumped into the cubbyhole, the wall felt wet and freezing cold even though it was summertime. Ian was grabbing hold of the rail at the other side of the enclosure, his face looking back at me with an expression of excitement and terror.

'I think I'm going to pee myself.' He said.

We wedged ourselves in and I managed to get a grip on one of the metal rails the train noise growing louder and I could feel a wind around us building more and more. I looked at the wall and could see writing in chalk:

Five Still Missing

'What does that mean?' I said to Peter but he was more interested in the 'Inter City 125' train approaching. The air pressure crept around my legs and upwards through my body like stepping into the sea, I was terrified. Before I could change my mind about the whole thing it was there, that enormous train approaching us. I peeked a look and saw a yellow flash, the front of the engine and then the high pitched whine from the tracks made me keep my eyes shut and hold onto the bar rail until my fingers ached from the grip.

The noise of the train pounded me against the wall like a wave and it felt like it was never going to stop. Then there was some shouting in my ear, Peter yelling about another train from the other direction on the adjacent tracks. The wailing began, the ghost boy was about to appear, I was convinced but I couldn't bring myself to look. After ten seconds I could hear someone calling my name over the noise.

I looked up to see the train motionless and inside was Kane grinning at me, swinging on the emergency chord; it hung down like a hangman's noose. The twins had vanished and Kane pointed down to the side door of the carriage, which gave a huge squeal and flew open creaking and banging on its hinges. I could see smoke coming from inside and then a foot appeared on the top of the metal steps. I walked out of the cubbyhole onto the gravel towards the train carriage, the smoke cleared and I could see another foot then a leg as the occupant lowered themselves down, jumping the last few feet onto the track. The figure was silhouetted at first and I struggled to make out who it was though they looked familiar. I stepped closer and then froze.

'Adam?'

It was my brother, he moved slower and awkwardly. As I ventured a bit closer still I could see that something wasn't quite right about him, his skull was bloodied, like at the graveyard and his neck was out of line so it kinked and his head swayed.

'Adam, can you see me?'

There was a banging noise, the train shunted forward and I looked up to see Kane waving at me from the window, I looked back at Adam but he was gone, inside again, waving at me. I ran towards the carriage, I wasn't afraid; he was still my brother. The train began to retreat into the tunnel and I caught hold of the metal step, pulling myself up as it rolled, trying not to get caught in the huge wheels beneath me. I used the door to manoeuvre myself up into the carriage and rolled in.

Kane was at the far end, staring out into the tunnel and I could see the back of Adam's head where he had lolled down in a seat, it was caked in blood and under the flickering light I realised the horse had virtually kicked the top of his head off during the accident. I fought the nausea rising from my belly and sat down on the nearest seat and waited.

Wherever that train was going, I was on it.

CHAPTER TEN

After a few minutes we reached the other end of the tunnel, the grey overcast daylight felt alien and new to me like it was going to tear at the horizon and unravel any second. I blinked and when I opened my eyes again Kane and Adam were walking along a wooden platform outside. I got out and followed them across a wooden bridge and onto a muddy track road, horse drawn carriages passed us as we neared a small town.

I ran up to Kane with Adam hobbling slowly behind, he didn't even acknowledge me. Kane grabbed me by the collar.

'Don't you be offended, he's in a different place to us that's all.'

'Where are we?'

'Gallows Close.'

'No we're not. I don't recognise any of this.'

Kane led me into a courtyard. People milled around dressed in similar clothes to him, like extras from a show my mum watched on a Sunday evening. It was boring on the screen but seeing it like this blew my mind. Besides Adam was there too. He might not see me but he was there with me, my brother.

'Davy, this is Gallows Close in the year Seventeen Fifty,' Said Kane 'the reign of George the second.'

'How?'

'Never mind *how*. Do you want to see where your house gets built?'

I nodded slowly, the faces of the people passing blurring, I thought they were staring at me but when I turned to look up they would spin away quickly and avoid my gaze.

We stopped in a huge courtyard with a large well in the

middle, horse drawn carriages rumbled past, people milling about. Wherever I was I could smell the world around me, feel the air and see it in it's greying tint.

'That's it, across the way there, where the jail is, that becomes your house. Across the alleyway to the left is the Inn, which becomes Carl's house. Now if you go down that alleyway in-between you can see why the close got its name.'

'There's nothing there.'

'Further Davy.'

Kane prodded me in the back and we walked to the large gap between buildings then forwards into the alleyway. The sky seemed to shrink in on us as we entered. The buildings creaked and hummed from activity inside, they were imposing and frightened me, I could see shadows through the misty windows of the Inn on the left, people snatching glances back at us behind candle lit portals. On the right the jail windows were barred, the odd face pressed up against it.

'Come here son. I have to tell you somethin.' Said one of them, his arm edging between two iron bars into the alleyway towards me.

'Don't look at them Davy, keep walking.'

I felt a cold wind biting into my face and hands and wanted to go home. The heavens opened in a cracking great thunderclap and rain beat down upon us in the muddy alleyway.

'I want to go back now.'

'You can't. Look you're almost there.'

Under the moonlight as if in a spotlight it rose up from a platform, a single thick vertical structure. Then, as we neared another lightning flash lit it up again and I could make out another part, a short horizontal section coming out.

'What is it?'

'Gallows.'

'It looks like the game we used to play in the car Adam. Remember Hangman?'

I turned round to look for him but Adam was still far behind in the alleyway, catching up with us.

'Can he hear me?'

Kane put his arm on my shoulder.

'He knows you're here, he just can't tune into your wavelength.'

I got closer to the steps that led to the platform and gingerly walked up. I could smell something pungent now, stale air like rust and dirty rain water. There was a knocking noise underneath the platform.

'Davy, come away from there.' Kane said.

'Why?'

'It's enough to see it for now but don't get too close. Come away.'

The ground shook and I heard sounds from below the gallows, under the platform, sobbing and cries of despair.

'Is this where they hang people?' I said, jumping down into the muddy courtyard.

'If they catch you.' He smiled at me.

'Have you ever been caught?'

'No, because I ran from the right things but I didn't run from my destiny. You'll spend your life running from shadows if you don't deal with your destiny.'

The rain started to get heavier and I felt soaked through, my clothes sticking to me, Kane was standing by a wooden cart; there was a tarpaulin heavy blanket over it and the stench was making me gag.

'Come and see what I have here.'

'I need to go now, please.'

'You need to know why you feel the way you do.'

'My head hurts, I want to go home now please.' I began to back down the alley towards the courtyard.

He pulled the blanket away, a swarm of flies hurtled up into the air, the shape of a person, thousands of them and the stench of the body underneath hit me again. It looked burnt and was in such a state I couldn't pick out any features.

'Don't you want justice?' Kane pointed across the yard, I turned and saw Adam walking up the other steps on the far side of the Gallows, dragging his feet and stumbling to stay straight.

'I want to go home.'

I turned and headed down the alleyway, the Jail and the Inn seemed to be closer together, I was starting to bash into them, more and more as I tried to reach the Courtyard until I was squeezing between them and breathing in to move an inch. I remembered the waste crusher in *Star Wars* and wanted Adam to come and help me, rescue me, he must still have recognised his little brother, the one he'd saved once.

A hand came out from the jail window and pulled at my clothes.

'I need to tell you something.' Came the rasping voice.

I pulled myself free.

'Stop digging while you can.'

I gave a big push and popped out from between the buildings into the courtyard like a cork from a bottle.

The well in the middle of the courtyard was static but the actual ground surrounding it was spinning like a slow playing record. I got to my feet and tried to run but I wasn't going anywhere. Kane was stood on top of the well as I circled him.

'You can't get off *this* ride Davy. You can't run forever.'

A horse and cart hurtled past. A dog appeared beside it, it looked like Bilbo. The driver reached down and cursed me with his riding stick waving it inches from my face. I looked up at him in his flailing cloak, face hidden by a large three-cornered hat.

'Stop digging.' He bellowed at me as he tried to strike me again, I closed my eyes as a high-pitched scream pierced my ears and the ground shook where I stood.

A lightning fork turned into flashing taillights as the train belted out of the tunnel leaving a gust of wind that wrapped around me like the tail of a dragon.

I was back in the tunnel.

'We did it Davy.' Ian screamed into my ears.

Carl was running towards us from across the track.

'That was amazing.'

I looked down the other end of the tunnel and saw another tiny light disappearing.

'You alright Davy?' Carl said.

I nodded slowly.

'Really? You look like you've shit yourself.'

I pushed past him and ran out of the tunnel.

CHAPTER ELEVEN

I woke up in my old bed and got up to go to the loo, stepping on my skateboard I went crashing into the back of the shelf unit.

'Davy what are you doing?' Shouted Mum from downstairs and for a moment I thought I was still ten years old. The pain going through my middle-aged head however reminded me that adults don't bounce when they fall.

I picked up some books I'd knocked down from the shelf. *Kidnapped* by Robert Louis Stevenson was open at a picture of Davy Balfour hiking across the Scottish moors. I flicked the book and was about to put it back on the shelf when I noticed a piece of paper, at first it looked like a bookmark but there was a poem on it. As I read the italic inky words I realised it wasn't just a poem, it was the lyrics we adapted into The Sleeping Gallows the words had been given to me by Kane after one of our encounters. I'd found them in my pocket and a few years later used them in an idea for the song which I'd taken to Carl to work on together when we were starting a band.

> *'Midnight (?) on a trail of death,*
> *Waking from nightmares,*
> *Struggle (fight?) for breath...'*

I laughed at my teen-angst prose and placed it all back on the shelf thinking it was perhaps a useful bit of evidence when I caught up with Carl and challenged him about the song. Pulling on my jeans and T-shirt I made my way downstairs. Horace was reading a paper, Mum stood at the cooker.

'Morning.' He said in a jolly voice.

'Is it?' I sat down, my hair a mess.

'Did you sleep well Davy?' Said Mum.

'Sort of. Had some old dreams.'

'Always were a dreamer that was half the problem I hear.' Horace mumbled.

'Who asked you?' I said as Mum returned to the cooker.

'What's that?'

I scowled at Horace who looked pretty pleased with himself.

'I was referring to nightmares.'

'Don't tell me, Gallows. Highwaymen? You were obsessed.'

'I haven't had that dream since I left though.'

'She'll be taking you back to that Doctor if you don't snap out of it.' Horace said, tapping his pipe on the edge of the table.

Mum put a grilled breakfast on the table. Horace lent in to grab some of my fried bread.

'Haven't had this in a while.' He said, crunching it.

I tucked in like an animal, stopping after a while to look up at the disapproving faces. I'd really let myself go in the last few years but I was surviving, I'd had no time for manners and etiquette when I was living the way I did. I didn't like it much but I'd had nobody to challenge me. Perhaps coming back would get me back into normal habits, whatever *normal* was.

'You look like you need a shave. I'll wash your clothes if you leave them on your bed.' Said Mum.

'There's no need. '

'You obviously lost your sense of smell on your travels those trousers stink of rainwater. Either you let me wash them or you can sleep in the shed.'

We sat there quietly for a while, I drank a pot of tea and sat back feeling bloated.

'So when did you last hear from Dad?'

'I was going to ask you the same thing.' Mum said, picking up the plates.

'Still in Canada?'

'I thought you would have made more of an effort to stay in touch. I don't hear much from him just the occasional Christmas card.'

I had visited my Dad once in Canada when I was on tour with a band, it was for a few days and I had hoped to feel the closeness we'd once had but after Adam died things had changed, he had become more withdrawn and often vanished up to bed complaining of a migraine.

'I was thinking of going to see Loz.'

'That will be nice.'

Mum went over to a draw and pulled out a mobile phone.

'Here, it's Stuart's old phone. Needs a charge but it works, unless you've got one already?'

'No, no I can't stand the things but it could be handy while I'm back here.'

'Here, take this as well.'

She prized open her purse and threw down fifty pounds.

'Spend it wisely, I don't have much these days.'

'Mum, you don't have to give me this.'

'I know but I can treat my son can't I?'

I looked up at her and realised that I'd missed out on so many years of our relationship that I'd never get back. Still, you have to live your own life and often I felt I was living for two, Adam and me. He never got to experience much so perhaps that excused my excesses. I certainly felt he'd been watching over me and guiding me through some tight spots over the years.

I asked Mum if she knew where Carl was. She wasn't too sure but it raised the sensitive topic of his parent's deaths.

'Sat on by an Elephant.' Horace pronounced like he was

auditioning for King Lear. 'I had a similar thing happen in Madagascar with a Zebra.'

'Sat on by an Elephant.' Mum echoed.

Carl's parents had been very unlucky. They had inherited a sum of money from Carl's Grandfather and taken early retirement. They moved to a new estate and treated themselves to a world tour getting as far as Thailand when they took a ride through the jungle on Elephants. On the last morning the guide was trying to organise the animals for the trek that day and just as they passed Carl's folks tent he had seen a snake. He tried to bat it away with a stick but it got the better of him and bit him so he flapped around startling the elephants and one of them sat down on Carl's parent's tent, squashing them flat.

'At least it was quick.' My mum had said down the transatlantic line. *'Are you coming back for the funeral, Carl's in a right state?'* I never did and it was something I'd felt bad about but what could I have done from Canada where I was on tour at the time? I sent a card although I never had enough for a stamp so I hoped it got there. There was a part of me that hoped at the time Carl would now understand how much losing Adam had hurt. I was into *'Karma'* at that point in my life.

'Loz might know where he is now.' Said Mum.

She left the room, taking some washing out into the back garden. I looked at Horace who was tapping his pipe and looking very smug.

'Horace, maybe we got off on the wrong foot.'

He stopped tapping and raised an eyebrow.

'You think so?'

'This is weird for me.'

'Go on.'

'I really am interested in your house.' I said.

'Yes?'

'The gallows, that's where it was, was that why nobody built on it?'

He put the newspaper down and his eyebrows launched up towards his swept over fringe.

'The Georgian highwayman told you that?'

'And who might that be?'

'I think you know Davy. Sounds to me like you know very well indeed of our Mr Balfour.'

He held his gaze and I waited for him to slip into a laugh but it never came. I was used to staring people out but I had to look away, he was giving me the creeps. I knew this was potentially a pisstake at my dreams and that Mum had told him about Kane.

'Have you met him?' I said.

'Met him?' Horace laughed. He was an ancestor of a cousin who decided robbery was much better than an honest days work. He hung for it you know.'

'No he didn't he never got caught.'

'Ah so you really have met him then.' Horace looked pleased with himself. I wasn't sure if this was a double bluff now or for real.

'Is that tomb at the graveyard his?'

Horace padded fresh tobacco into his pipe and lit it thoughtfully.

'Perhaps we should have a chat when you've reunited with the others, the five of you back together.'

CHAPTER TWELVE

As I strolled across the road in the daylight I got a better look at Horace's house. It stood out with its brickwork and feathered patterns above the windows. I wondered who had agreed to its construction at the council but I suppose if he was an ancestor then he was entitled to do what he wanted with it.

I reached Loz's gate. Years melted away as I remembered opening it a hundred times during those hot school holidays. *'Can Loz come out to play?'* I'd say as I quivered on the step. The strictest parent in the Close was always Loz's mum. Most of the mums would give you cakes and let you mess around in the house but she would hit you with a hairbrush and chase you as soon as look at you for the slightest misdemeanour. She counted a lot too, always counting things or washing her hair up to five times a day. They call it obsessive-compulsive disorder now. Once she found Loz stealing her cigarettes and made him smoke the whole packet until he puked then eat the contents of the ash tray. That was what he told us although I think he made the last bit up.

I knocked at Loz's house and luckily his mum was out, even decades on it made me shudder to remember her. Loz answered in a face mask, the kind they start wearing when a flu pandemic is on the news.

'Davy! Your mum told me you were back.'

'What's with the Michael Jackson look?' I said.

'Been cleaning, come in and wipe your feet. In fact here put these on.' He handed me some little white mitts. 'Stick those on your feet.'

'You're joking.'

'No, come on hurry up and close the door.'

I walked into the room and slipped the tiny elastic paper covers onto my shoes. It was always minimalist inside but now it was clinical in its sparsity like a medical clean room.

'Mum's out.'

'Erm, well I was a bit nervous to tell you the truth. No hairbrushes lying around I hope?'

'Blimey I remember that, no she mellowed quite a bit, well they found the right medication basically. Still has 'episodes' but rarely, I run a tight ship here.'

'And your Dad?'

'He's fine. Plays golf mostly and I tend to manage the house, cook and clean.'

'Loz the domesticated diva, you always did well at helping your mum with the cakes didn't you?

'What are you getting at?'

'Just put the kettle on will you.' I said.

'You haven't changed much.' He said, going into the kitchen and wiping the taps before filling the kettle.

'I would actually beg to differ when I look in the mirror.' I said, catching my reflection in the stainless steel toaster.

'What brings you back after so long?'

'Mixture of stuff I guess.'

'Carl got something to do with it?'

'Why do you say that?'

'Come on Davy, you two never sorted it out. Bloody hell the crap you went through.'

'Partly to see Carl, to be honest I got sick of running.'

'Well it's good to see you.' He said.

'You fancy a stroll up the woods after this, thought we could check out the old stomping ground.'

'Not really.'

'Come on it'll be a laugh.'

'Ah, the new road ruined it Davy. It's not the same place

over there.'

'You remember being in that tunnel?'

Loz offered me some ginger nut biscuits. I took three as he made the tea in a golf ball shaped chrome sieve.

'We must have been mad, could have killed one of us so easily messing around in there with the trains.'

'Nah, we were charmed.'

'*You* thought you were, you and the highwayman watching over you.'

I stared at the floor and wondered whether I should tell Loz that the dreams were coming back. We all used to take the piss out of each other over various things and that became my theme. I decided to pass for now.

'So who else have you seen?' He said, handing me my drink.

'I was going to look the twins up.' I soaked all three biscuits into the mug then stuffed them into my mouth. Loz lent over with a small plate to catch the crumbs.

'They both got married and live pretty close. Ian's wife Liz is a bit scary but Peter married a gorgeous girl called Susie. She used to be in our school, a few years younger. Both got kids now.'

I wiped my mouth with my sleeve and looked at him. His mask slung around his neck on elastic.

'You fancy a trip to see them with me?'

'I have stuff to do Davy.'

'Come on, twenty-five years, let's go see them.' I pressed.

'Well I *do* see them, they visit their folks and come over.'

'You got their address for me?'

He walked over to the phone unit and took out a book flicking through it. The smell of disinfectant was overwhelming. Loz handed me a post-it note with an address on.

'Sure you won't come?'

'It's a long story but I'm happier staying right here Davy. Sorry.'

'Okay. And what about Carl. You seen him?'

'Not much, he hasn't been back since they sold his folks place.'

'Any numbers I could try?'

'No but I e-mailed him on a networking site, he's got a fan page.'

'He has fans now, what a joke, did he reply?'

'Not yet but he's probably busy. He's doing really well since he wrote those songs.'

'I know and one of them is mine, well half mine and I want some royalties while I'm here.'

Loz's face changed.

'That's why you came back isn't it? Not out of any sense of nostalgia, or because you were missing us.'

'Of course I missed you mate.'

He seemed angry with me, avoiding my gaze.

'I can't go back and change things Loz. People move away, that's life.'

'Yeah and then come back when they want something.'

'I'm here now, why the grilling, I thought you'd be pleased to see me?'

'You're going to do more than ask Carl for money aren't you?' He looked at me like he suddenly didn't recognise me. I put my hand on his shoulder, he checked the clock on the wall and moved towards the door.

'Davy I need to get on, I'll see you out.'

'What do you mean *do more*?'

He held his hand out for my mug.

'I haven't finished my tea yet.'

'You can bring the mug back later I've got a conference call in five minutes.'

'I can wait if you want to come out later to see the twins?'

'I can't. Don't keep on about it.'

'Loz, are you avoiding going out?'

'I can't sodding go out.'

'What do you mean, ASBO tag?' I laughed.

Loz dropped his shoulders and lent on the hallway wall.

'I'll get to the front garden and...' he trailed off.

'And what?'

'I freeze, like when some people try to get up a ladder and just cease up for no reason.'

'You're taking the piss?'

'I can't seem to control it.'

'For Gods sake Loz, you're winding me up right?'

'No. It's been getting worse for years.'

'Agoraphobia? Bollocks, just come out with me.'

'No. Look Davy, its fine for you but you don't understand. Can you just leave it?'

I could see he was starting to actually sweat and get really agitated.

'Yeah, yeah look I'm sorry it's been weird coming back and I'm trying to adjust you know?' I took a swig of my tea as I stepped outside.

'Good luck finding Carl. Maybe he does owe you for stealing Charlotte away and using that song but...'

'But?'

'He didn't mean what happened with Adam. It was an accident.'

'You think I want to kill him?' I said.

'It was an accident Davy.'

'Well I was the only one who was there that day.'

'It was an accident, leave the past where it is, please?'

He closed the door and I suddenly felt shit. I had really missed people over the years but you get used to it, you make new friends and time blurs it all until you set foot into their presence as I had just done and suddenly they were very real and it was a lie, of course you missed these people like mad because you shared so many special things that bonded you once upon a time. It wasn't that I didn't love them; it was just that we had ended up so far away. And why was he scared I wanted to do something bad to Carl, did he see something in me that I couldn't?

I sat on the kerb with my mug of tea and watched as some kids cycled past.

'Are you a homeless?' Said the little boy with his stabiliser wheels rattling. I recognised him from the day before in the rain.

'Who taught you manners?'

'You smell like my old dog.'

I made a barking noise and he started to laugh.

'Why are you here?'

'I used to live here.'

'Where?'

'Over there.' I said pointing to my house.

'Next to the haunted place?' He said.

'Haunted?' I said, surprised.

'The man said it was but we can't go in there.'

'What man?'

The boy's sister called over. She was outside Carl's old house next to where Horace now lived.

'Oliver come on we have to go in now.'

'I have to go.'

He pushed his pedals down and sped away with his little legs going ten to the dozen.

'Hey, what man told you all this?' I called after him. I looked past Oliver as he reached his driveway to the new house and saw Horace watching us from his front window.

CHAPTER THIRTEEN

A woman with neat bobbed hair opened the door holding a baby, two older children hiding behind her legs, curious to see who had been knocking. She looked at me in my beaten up jeans, unkempt hair and army coat.

'I told the other guy, we have some already.'

'Some what?'

'Whatever it is, drive, windows, dish cloths.

'Oh no, please I'm not selling anything.'

'I'll call the police.'

'But...'

'Kids get inside.'

'My name is...'

'Listen I don't care, how would you like me to interrupt your afternoon by trying to sell you a push chair or some half-baked religious claptrap?'

'I'll deal with it.' Came a familiar voice from behind her in the hallway.

Ian appeared and his mouth fell open.

'Bloody hell. Davy!'

'Hello Ian.'

'What the...?'

'Thought it was time I said hello.'

'Babe this is Davy.' Ian moved her to one side.

'The guy from the Close?' She said.

I looked at her expecting her to now seem really embarrassed and make a full apology.

'I see what you mean now.' With that she walked back inside.

'Oh mate it's so weird to see you.'

'Yeah, yeah it's been a while.' I said.

'Don't mind Liz, she's a bit spiky at first.' He laughed.

He ushered me inside and sat me down in the kitchen next to a baby in a high chair. I wasn't even sure if it was the same one as his wife was holding at the door, it was full of kids.

'Keep an eye on Jnr will you Ian.'

'*Jnr*' did a raspberry with his mouth and laughed at me and the other kids seemed to take to me, if you can count having toy cars being bounced off your head and the baby being sick on you.

Peter, the other twin lived within an hours drive so Ian called him straight away. He said that he'd be over later that afternoon and arrived with his three kids in tow and wife Susie who was the opposite of Liz, she cuddled me and told me she'd always wanted to meet the '*infamous Davy*' and I found out that she would sometimes pop into my mums with cakes.

I sat in the garden opposite the twins. The boys were identical in appearance, Peter was only minutes older than Ian but when you'd grown up with them you could tell the difference in seconds.

We chatted about what had happened since we'd last seen each other; the ease between old friends can transcend time. Sure we were older and uglier with more lines around the eyes, none more than me after the lifestyle I'd chosen but overall we'd fared reasonably well.

Ian went back inside to get some beers and put *The Sleeping Gallows* on. He walked out laughing and chucked the CD cover at me.

'You'll never guess who wrote this?'

'Me and Carl.' I said raising my glass.

They looked at each other then back at me.

'You wish. It's one of Carl's, I saw him on TV getting an award for it.'

'What?'

'Yeah he's done loads but this one must be one of those that set you up for life.'

I leant forwards.

'Boys, I wrote this song with Carl in eighty-five in your garage. You were both in the band for about a week.'

'Before you made us roadies!'

'I was looking around at the folks for that tape we made. I'm sure it's on there somewhere.' I said.

'I think I do remember a tape. Didn't we do something with it?' Ian said.

'It's really important that I find it. If Carl is like he used to be then he's not going to hand over half the royalties without a fight.'

'I've moved twice since then, there's no way we kept it.'

'You are serious, you wrote this with him?' Peter said.

'I *know* I wrote it.'

'So you haven't got hold of Carl yet?'

'I have a record company address so I'm going down to the city to see what I can find out.'

'You know what happened to his folk's right?'

'Mum wrote and told me.'

'That was the last time we saw him, at the funeral.'

'I couldn't get back in time.' I said.

'It was horrible,' Said Ian, 'they'd lost the bodies in some mix up over there and so Carl had empty coffins filled with bricks. He even got the weight right, it was the oddest funeral ever.'

Peter reached into his pocket and got out a pile of small photos from his wallet. He sifted through and handed me one, a faded seventies picture of the five of us in the Close on our skateboards, Loz, The Twins, Carl and me.

'We weren't much older than some of our kids when that

was taken.' He said.

'Must be thirty years ago.'

I held the picture closer. 'Hey I can see Adam in the background, just outside the disused plot.'

'I never noticed that before.' Peter said, taking it.

'Poor Adam.' Said Ian.

We sat there for a moment, none of us quite sure what to say, it had always been a touchy subject especially around me of course as I had found it so hard to come to terms with it being an accident.

'So how's it been going with your music Davy? I thought you were doing well in Japan according to your mum.'

'I did for a bit then the band split up. Japan isn't the cheapest place to live so I went to Malaysia and played in bars for a while, solo mostly then on to Oz and a bit in the States and managed to see dad when we played Canada. Then the gigs dried up, I had to play cover songs to get interest. Ended up in a Spanish resort.'

I flinched at the last one, remembering what had happened over the last month there and how low I'd sunk from the peak of my fifteen minutes of success in the band.

'They found that bloke over there this week smashed up on the beach. Sounds bloody rough out there.'

'It's getting worse here too.' Said Peter. That's why we moved further away from the city.

'That's why I stay away from the Cities, I bloody hate them. Give me space and some nice bars, long beaches any day.'

'But there's no work in places like that, only seasonal. I mean you're stuck to where the work is mostly in life.' Said Peter.

'At Davy went for it.' Ian said, 'I never got to travel that much, Liz wanted to get a house and then before we knew it the kids arrived not that I mind I mean I love those kids but I wish sometimes I'd travelled a bit first.

'You're only forty now though, in ten or fifteen years they will be leaving home and you can do it all then.' I said.

'You mean when they go to college and want cars and fees and bailing out?' Peter laughed.

There was something about their lives I envied. Despite it looking like a ball and chain sometimes it must have been nice to have kids to come home to, to be excited to see you and give you a hug before dragging you outside to kick a football about. Dad had been like that with Adam and me.

'You never had any kids yourself then?' Said Ian.

'You know what they say about rock and rollers mate, *'not to my knowledge.'* I held my hands up.

'So have you been over the tunnel woods yet?'

'No, I was hoping we could go over there together for a nose about, take a few beers or something?'

'Yeah maybe an extra can for your mate?'

They started to laugh.

'What's so funny?'

'You used to have that invisible friend?'

'Kane' said Peter.

'We were young and there *was* a Kane buried up there in that Churchyard.'

They laughed again, they did it in offbeat sync like a piston engine and it drove me mad.

'Alright guys, easy now.'

'Maybe it really was a haunted plot of land where the Gallows stood?' Peter said.

'What's to say there weren't Gallows there, the name must have come from somewhere.'

They looked at each other and shrugged. They never had taken it very seriously; they had been spooked a bit when

I told them as kids but we were camping in the woods and anything seemed scary when we did that.

'Did you ever forgive Carl for stealing Charlotte away?'

'You remembered that too?' I said, trying to hide the sudden twisting inside my guts. I had been besotted with Charlotte.

'You were crushed.'

'I don't remember it bothering me that much.' I lied.

They looked at each other and raised their eyebrows.

'Anyway I'm back to see you idiots and sort this song business out first.'

Peter looked at the kids bouncing around in a caged trampoline. 'Come on, let's have a go.' He walked over and persuaded the kids to take a break. They watched us all get on there with bewilderment and we started to bounce around.

'I bet I can do a higher roll than you.' Said Peter to Ian.

'I bet I can do one higher.' Said Ian pushing him and wobbling about and crashing into the sidebars to stabilise himself.

'Do you reckon Davy can still wrestle like Hulk Hogan?' They both said in unison.

'Blimey, nothing changes does it?' I said, knowing what was coming next.

'Bundle!' Shouted Peter bouncing over and knocking me into the netting and trying to put me in a headlock. Ian took my legs and I wriggled around while the kids and wives looked on.

No matter how much time passed the kids you grew up with stood as a great leveller. I hoped somehow that Carl had grown into a more reasonable adult but I had my doubts. It had only taken minutes before the twins, Loz and I had reverted to type so why should he be any different?

CHAPTER FOURTEEN

I got off the packed train at the city station and headed to the address of the company who released *The Sleeping Gallows*. I soon realised why the faces in my carriage had been so long and miserable. Even before we got to the ticket machines people were jostling and pushing to get ahead. I elbowed a guy in a suit who had cut me up as I waited my turn.

'You want to say 'excuse me pal?' I said, glaring at him.

'Welcome to the City.' He muttered as someone barged past the two of us. Being courteous there was like trying to swim against a strong tide.

As I walked up the dirty concrete steps into the streets it didn't get much better, the traffic, the crowds and the smell made me feel sick. I'd been too used to warmer climates, holiday resorts and travelling big countries, I'd forgotten what it was to be a pack rat squirming for air and space.

Carl went under the name of *'Carl Garl'* when he wrote or performed. Apparently it was what his little sister called him when she was first trying to talk. This wouldn't sound strange except Carl and his sister hated each other ever since the *'Bilbo bit me'* incident. At the time she was also trying to nurse a hawk that had fallen out of its nest on top of the train chimney that stood in the vacant plot. Every day she would go and creep through the fence and check on the wounded creature taking a cup of milk. She would happily sit there chatting away to it and it got stronger and started to trust her even eating from her palm. One day she arrived to find that Carl had put a full stop to the recovery and kicked it to death to get back at his sister. He was given the slipper by his dad and grounded for a month, we should have seen it in him then, the merciless streak that ran through lots of his acts.

At least he hadn't become a vet I thought as I arrived outside the huge skyscraper. It took me a lifetime to walk through the revolving glass doors, a vast atrium, and finally reach the semi-circled reception desk. All under the watchful gaze of the security guards. The receptionist's hair was so tightly pulled into a bun on top of her head that it made her look like a giant onion.

'Morning, I wonder if you can help me, I'm looking for Carl Garl.'

'Do you have an appointment?'

'Not exactly, you can tell him Davy is here to see him I'm sure he'll be happy to see me.'

She looked me up and down and couldn't hide the disdain as her mouth twitched and gave it away. Body language often speaks louder than words. I subtly inhaled to check that I had washed that day.

'Davy who?'

'Just say Davy, he'll know. Or say Davy and Kane, he'll laugh at that.' I draped myself over the counter confidently and smiled my best smile at her but the ice maiden wasn't melting. She pressed a few buttons on her keyboard.

'He doesn't actually work here today but I can leave a message with one of the associates.'

'Aw. Shame. Can you tell me *where* he is or give me a mobile, it's kind of important?'

'I'm sorry we can't give out that sort of information.'

'Look I've come a long way to see him, from across the ocean.'

She looked over at Security and one of the three guys in grey starchy outfits walked over. He was a little taller than me but I reckoned I could handle him if I had too. Security guards weren't always as eager to get into fights as nightclub bouncers, that was something I'd learnt too.

'This man is refusing to leave.' She said.

'Why did you say that?' I turned to her and she gave a tight-lipped smile. 'I just want to see Carl Garl, he knows me we grew up together.'

'I'm sorry but you'll have to leave Sir.'

'Sir? Oh that's nice. I'm a *Sir* but I have to leave?' The guard stepped closer and I held my hands up. I was eyeing up the lift behind him. I noticed a plaque with the record company logo I'd seen on the Internet. That was the floor I needed to get to.

'Give me a break will you, just a number or some way to reach him?'

He shook his head so I shrugged and walked back to the revolving doors, the receptionist took an incoming call. I did a little Superman act in the doors, exiting and then back inside three sixty degrees, striding over to the lift.

The receptionist glanced up and called out but I'd darted across to the lift as it was closing. The people inside looked at me, nervous due to the fact there was a guard running towards us. I hammered on the button for the seventeenth floor and watched his frustrated face outside the glass elevator as it shot up through the tubular shaft. I gave him a little wave but I knew my time was limited and I had to locate Carl quickly.

The seventeenth floor was a lush office with enough plants in the hallway to leave David Bellamy salivating. I marched down the corridor and found another glass panel door, it was locked and on the other side was a desk and a woman, she looked friendlier than Miss Onion Bun-head on reception but wasn't responding to my knocking on the toughened glass door. Then she picked up her phone, looked at me, surprised then a bit concerned and grinned. I wasn't sure if it was fear or happiness really on her face. I banged on the door again.

'I'm here to see Carl Garl.' I expect through the glass door this sounded like *'grrr grrr'*.

There was a buzzing then a ping and I thought that the door was about to open but it was the lift behind me. I turned to see the guard and his two friends. I bolted to the stairs door but I had barely opened it before they grabbed me.

'Look, I don't want to....'

Nobody listens to me when this happens. If you've ever given any security force folk a reason to put you in an arm lock you'll know how good they are at it. One minute you think they're giving you a friendly arm over shoulder thing like your Dad did when you were a kid wrestling in the garden then the next you are involuntarily being guided diagonally towards the floor.

'Oh nice carpet, I think it's the same twill as my old apartment.' I said.

In this peculiar position I was escorted to the lift and taken down to the reception. The receptionist looked delighted, almost as if she wanted them to hold me so she could take a freebie kick in the groin. I was unceremoniously ejected through a door to the side of the revolving one, an emergency door to my relief as initially I thought they were putting me through the front window Jackie Chan style. I stumbled and did a funny Norman Wisdom trip, managed to steady myself and then wrapped myself around a bin.

'Wankers!' I shouted.

A few people stopped and were watching as the guards stood in a line by the door.

'The Sleeping Gallows is one of mine.'

'That's nice for you dear.' Said a little lady with a tiny dog.

Most passers-by circumnavigated me without getting too close. I was pushing my hand through my hair and trying to regain some sort of composure, half-laughing, half-crazy with anger. It wasn't a good look.

'That's right have a good stare.'

I could hear a police siren in the distance and not wanting to have any more twisty-arm games with the big nasty men I decided to get out of there.

* * *

I walked back through the busy streets, thousands of stranger's faces flashing by me, none of them offering so much as a glance or a smile. As I neared the train station I felt for the money in my pocket, I still had the best part of forty pounds left and all the stress had made me hungry. I stopped outside one of those new places that try to look traditional and warm but end up like a theme park restaurant.

I went in and ordered a burger and a pint while I figured out my next move. Carl was so important now that I couldn't even get to see him? I'd soon fix that.

'You better get ready you piece of scum.' I muttered. I looked up and saw that a few people at the bar were watching me. I smiled at them.

'Don't mind me.'

I ordered at the bar and sat down by the window watching the city rolling on. They had now banned cigarettes in pubs which was good for someone who'd quit his twenty a day habit but instead you got a strong whiff of beer soaked carpets and the bogs wreaked, especially in the older venues.

The waitress came over with my burger. I smiled and said thank you but she'd barely let it hit the table before zipping away again without acknowledging me.

'Have a nice day to you too.'

She hadn't bothered with cutlery either, so I walked over to the bar and asked how I was going to eat my salad without it. The barman just stared blankly then pointed to a condiment trolley.

'Always a pleasure, never a chore.' I said, shaking my head at a drinker perched on his stool. He had a trilby hat on and an old suit like Horace wore, he would have looked more at home in a speakeasy in the thirties.

'Is service always this good or did I just get lucky?' I said. He stared at his drink and ignored me.

The cutlery was old and dirty and I ended up using my overcooked burger to scoop up some of the limp salad that was like a tissue in a hailstorm.

As I was nearing the end of my fourth pint in an hour I decided I should leave while I still had my faculties and enough money for the bus at the other end. The food deal wasn't a bad price but the drink on its own was five times what I had been paying abroad.

The lone drinker at the end of the bar suddenly decided to buy me a drink. I'd forgotten he was there, reading his paper with his trilby tucked down I thought he was asleep resembling a pile of second hand clothing.

'Cheers. Nice to know there's some friendly faces in this hole.' I said, ordering a large scotch. It felt sharp after the bitter beer but it gave me a head rush as I sat back down.

'Good health Davy.' He said, not looking up from underneath his hat.

Before I realised he'd used my name *The Sleeping Gallows* came on the stereo.

'Hey can you change the station?' I shouted out to the bar. Nobody paid any attention to me. 'I said can you change the

station?' I stamped about snapping my fingers.
The barman broke off from his conversation.

'No. It is satellite.' He said in a thick accent.

'What do you mean?'

'It is broadcast to all the pubs in the chain.'

'Well think for yourself for once and break the chain. I'm a paying customer.'

'Okay enough drink for you I'm going to ask you to leave please.'

'Why, it's not exactly like I'm using up space in your empty pub is it and I know for a fact you wouldn't be so rude if you knew who wrote this song.'

He shook his head and looked at the two men at the bar. The man who had bought the drink for me piped up.

'I hate to burst your bubble but Carl Garl wrote this, he used to come in here and sit and write, just over in the corner there.'

'Well I hate to pop your bubble mate but I wrote this song.' I continued, 'and when I get the royalties it certainly won't be a celebration in this pub, want to know why?'

I got up and looked at the barman. 'Because you are rude, your waitress is rude.' I paused, looking around. 'He's alright at the end there.'

One of the men by the bar said something under his breath.

'What did you say?' I leered at him.

The barman reached over and grabbed my arm.

'He said there is nobody now please leave.'

I looked along the bar and the figure had gone, there was just a newspaper laid out on the bar.

'He's gone for a piss probably.' I said, blowing a raspberry as I staggered down to where he had been sitting, trying to read the headline on the paper that had been left open.

'*Police hunt British man over resort attack.*'

I leant on it to read more but it slid away quickly, I reached to catch it but instead I took a slow buckling dive towards the floor. I tried to grab at the stool but it was very polished wood, hard maple probably and it tumbled with me. I hit the floor with a thump and it was surprisingly comfortable so I decided to stay there a little longer, until I felt like getting up, or until the mystery drink buyer returned to buy another for me, or until I got thrown out.

It seemed to be the latter.

CHAPTER FIFTEEN

The gainfully employed of the city were heading home and I was staggering around like a gleeful moron hassling them to cheer the hell up.

'Get lost ya bum.' Said one of them.

'Shut up you miserable ol' git.' I shouted after him.

A mother covered her kid's ears and I curtseyed. The boy laughed at me.

'Sorry malady, I'm sure he's heard far worse on his computer games.'

I decided to get a strong coffee in a dodgy looking fast food place called *'Take Bap'*. I sat on the plastic seat and got myself together a bit, mumbling as I often did when I'd had a few. Carl would have loved to have seen me like that, totally shit faced in the daytime with little money in my pocket and him sat there in his ivory tower, counting the royalties from our record.

'Yeah you can laugh you penis head.' I muttered into my drink.

'Who are you talking to?' A woman's voice.

I looked up to see a woman smiling at me from another table. She was punky with coloured strips of extensions through her raven hair and skinny pale arms that had faded tattoos. She was a bit younger than me, probably in her late thirties. I waved back with a royal gesture and pulled my collar up, huddling over my hot drink.

'I was talking to my little cup here.'

She picked up her book and stuffed it into a furry pink shoulder bag then came and sat next to me.

'Someone sitting there.' I said. 'Bugger off.'

'Really?'

'Well, no but I do want to be left alone please.'

'Rough day?'

'Could say that.'

'Ah. Well you've got company now.'

'I'm not interested in any funny business.' I said.

She laughed a hearty loud laugh. 'I'm not a prostitute you cheeky wanker.'

'Sorry I didn't mean it like that.'

'Yes you did.' She said, retrieving a small bottle from her bag.

'Here,' she said tipping some of it into my coffee. 'Make you feel better.'

'I don't think I should have any more to drink you fat poof.'

'I beg your pardon?'

'See. I've had way too much already.' I giggled and a bit of snot flew out my nose, I wiped at it with my sleeve.

'Calypso coffee. Perk you right up.' She whispered, putting her hand onto mine.

The Sleeping Gallows came over the tinny radio.

'Oh no for Gods sake not again.' I slammed the table then dropped my face into my open palms. The owner looked over and told me to behave. I waved back and apologised in my slurring tones.

'I know, its shit isn't it.' She said. 'Life.'

'No it's not life that's shit, it's this song.'

'Yeah, who writes this bollocks?'

'It's mine it just needs a re-work.'

'You wrote this shit?'

'Yeah.'

'Shit.'

'Stop saying shit it's becoming nonsensical.' I said.

'Huh?'

I checked around for anyone listening.

'What's your name?'

'Petra.'

'Nice name. Do you believe in ghosts Petra?'

'Well I used to but the older I get the more I think we invent them ourselves.'

'Yeah?'

'I reckon it's a manifestation of a deep issue.'

'I think I've had too much to drink to understand what you just said.'

I started to tell her my story, strangers are good for that. We sat there for about an hour and she kept me in coffee with secret tipples of Tia Maria. Things got a bit hazy, when we left it was dark, we ate again at a pizza stand then I remember vaguely watching a band in a pub and buying drinks. I think at some point I was sick but it didn't stop my companion pulling my trousers down in the hallway of the squat where she lived and doing rude things to me before I passed out.

* * *

I woke up with a pair of feet on the pillow next to me; the toenails were painted different colours. Across the room was a scruffy looking bloke with long braided hair and a plastic toy Police helmet perched on top of his head, he was grinning at me and nodding as he sucked on a bong.

'Morning all.' He wheezed holding the tube towards me.

I shook my head.

He grinned at me and exhaled a long plume of smoke into the room. It filtered through the sunshine breaking into the torn curtains forming a dusty ray.

'You were wasted last night.' He said.

'I can't remember much. Got any speed?'

'Sorry man.'

'Coffee?'

'Kitchen's through there help yourself.'

I went into the kitchen and found a mug among the stack of pots and there was just enough coffee in the bottom of the jar. I splashed my face in the sink while waiting for the saucepan to boil and nosed about. The place was a mess and the fridge was like a shrine to Louis Pasteur. On the faded door were hundreds of those little magnetic words, mixed up to make sentences. I started to idly play about with some then I noticed three of them placed in the corner:

five still missing

I stared at them and for some reason I could hear them being whispered over and over in my head like it should mean something. The saucepan boiled over and fizzed breaking my train of thought and I poured what was left into the cup of stale coffee.

Upon returning to the other room I found Mr Dreads now in bed kissing Petra the punk.

'Er, what do you think you're doing?' I said.

He grinned at me then carried on kissing her as she stirred then the penny dropped.

'Petra is your girlfriend?'

'We bring back presents for each other now and then.'

'Well that's very nice, now can someone tell me where the hell I am?'

'You are wherever you want to be.' Petra said propping herself up on one elbow.

I downed my coffee and found my shoes; I wasn't getting much sense out of these two idiots.

'Ah, you can't go yet.' She purred up at me. 'Why don't you

join us for breakfast?'

She looked pretty sexy lying there half naked, her arms stretching out to me, breasts popping out over a purple wasp corset.

'I'll tell you what we *could* do.' I said, the nausea rising in my stomach as I felt my hangover kick in fully.

* * *

The gentle touch of sunshine warmed my face, it was a welcome jolt from the dope filled flat I'd just made a swift exit from. For a fleeting moment I'd considered her offer but then I changed my mind remembering the last time I'd tried it in Canada when I was touring. There was this gorgeous groupie called Lucinda who latched onto me and ended up travelling with us, I started to fall for her and thought we could get serious. When it came to sex however she was insistent this other guy Drew on the road crew had to join in for her to get her rocks off. It didn't do it for me, not seeing another blokes face peering at me from the other end of a female naked back. I'd panicked and ended up blabbing on about classic car engines that time. I found out that afterwards Drew was seeing her *one on one* and that was a bit of a blow for my ego and I also suspected he was responsible for one of my guitars going missing. I'd heard he was thrown off another tour for selling equipment for drugs. When I'd found out what was going on I had no option but to exact a little revenge so I surprised them one night in the tour bus bunks, took a few pictures of their shocked naked bodies and dumped them both off the tour.

* * *

I got some directions from a newsagent and strode towards the nearest station. I was still in the outskirts of the city, rows of houses and people walking dogs. After twenty minutes I reached the station and then my hope of a nice bath and change of clothing was swiftly dashed as I felt around in my pockets. The train ticket I'd purchased the day before had expired and the little change I had left had spilt out of my pockets at Petra's. There was no way I was going back there to that dirty slum, I would have to get another one.

I found Stu's old mobile phone and switched it on. It lit up briefly, made a huge farting sound as I put it to my ear and then died. It summed up my present situation.

I patted my hair down and started trying to explain my predicament to people as they came out the station emerging as fast as ball bearings from a scatter gun barrel. Most were too quick even for me to get a word in they were so keen to get to wherever it was they were headed.

'Yeah, you'll spend it on drink.' Said one chap in a nice suit.

'Get a job ya bum.' Said another in a long raincoat. I noticed he was the same bloke who I'd bumped into there the day before.

'What is this England or Chicago?' I shouted.

'Ah screw you creepo.' He gave me the finger.

'There's a shelter up that road.' A woman sweetly said to me.

'I'm not a homeless, I've just had a bit of a weird night.' I said as she walked on.

When I was travelling I used to sing for my supper so I wasn't embarrassed to have a go to raise a few quid. I began to sing some of the set I used to do, I had a reasonable singing voice and it was what people knew that got the money in especially when busking. I didn't have my guitar so I sort of clapped and stamped my feet on a manhole beneath me to get some rhythm.

After an hour I had managed to get about two pounds thirty-three and a sore leg. I'd even sung *The Sleeping Gallows* but city folk in the rush hour weren't the most captive audience and all the tourists wanted to do was have their picture taken with me like some freak attraction.

My leg hurt and so I sank down on an upturned milk crate and just held out my hand. In half an hour I managed to get up to four pounds and was almost halfway to my single fare back to the suburbs. It was warming up too and the sun had come out so I hoped people would start feeling more generous.

After another ten minutes a woman stopped, knelt down beside me and held out a hot coffee.

'It's a gingerbread latte if you fancy it?'

I looked up wondering if it had been a special order sent from above and there she was, looking as pretty as the day I'd last seen her all those years ago.

'Louise?'

'Davy? It *is* you.'

I had met Louise on a train in Malaysia several years previously, she'd divorced from a wealthy banker and I spent several weeks travelling with her. I did have a crush on her but felt I was punching above my weight to try it on especially with so much competition from toned musclemen along the beaches particularly *'Chuck'* who gave her a low room rate in his apartment block and I swear he used to charge me over the odds for mine when she managed to get me a room there too. Louise didn't seem to go for my rough rock star wannabe appearance so I was content with friendly banter and companionship.

To my amazement one evening she kissed me and we slept together in her apartment. For a week or so it was great but then Chuck began to hang around more and we had a row. Louise said that we were just lovers and she didn't want to feel like I owned her and that we should stop sleeping together if it was confusing me. I pretended it was cool but I knew that I was becoming too deeply involved and I suspected she had started to sleep with Chuck once we'd cooled things.

The next week I decided to move on before I fell in love with her. Sometimes a perfect memory is better than staying around to watch reality tear it down stone by stone.

'What happened to you in Malaysia?' She said.

'It's a long story, I'd buy you a coffee and tell you about it if I had any money but I seem to have acquired one for free now. Cheers.' I took a swig of her coffee; I could taste a hint of her lipstick from the rim.

'I had no idea where you went when you left me on my own.'

'You know me, like the littlest hobo. Keep moving on.' I knew at that moment that I probably smelt like him too.

'I got upset when you went I thought it was all the stuff that happened between us. I was in such a weird place back then after my divorce.'

'No harm done, it wouldn't have worked out between us anyway Lou, I mean I was into *Motorhead* and you were into all that *Durban Spiel*.'

'*Urban Chill!*' She laughed.

'Whatever it was there wasn't enough power chords.'

'Very funny, so it wasn't anything I did?' She said.

'No, it wasn't that, honest. Did you stay on there for a while?'

'Oh my God it was horrendous, you know they found one

of the lifeguards dead in the swimming pool?'

'What?'

'Chuck.'

'Thick neck Chuck?'

'Yeah.'

'Did they catch the person who did it?'

'What do you mean?'

'The killer.'

She looked at me confused for a moment. 'Oh no, he was pissed up or smoking some heavy weed that someone brought into the camp, went for a late night swim I think.'

'But you two were...?'

'No we weren't. Davy, you kept on about me having a thing for him.'

'Oh well, long time ago now.'

'It is but it's so good to see you Davy, I wish I wasn't in such a rush babe, can we meet up later?'

'I need to get home really first but I had a bit of a crazy night. Hence this situation I've found myself in.'

'You need money? Shit it's no hassle, how much do you need?' She said reaching into her bag.

'Just a tenner to get home. I do have a home don't worry.'

She handed me a twenty. 'You don't need to explain to me silly.'

'I'm going to get this back to you, write your number for me.'

'Really, don't sweat it.'

'I insist I have to pay you back and we can go for a meal or something.'

'Okay, you can find me here. We can hook up.' She handed me a card. It looked like she was doing well, some PR firm in the city and she had *'Director'* after her name.

'So where are you off to exactly?'

'To meet my boyfriend. In fact you could come to the party later we're having, would you like to?'

'Sure.' My heart sank a bit at the boyfriend news but at least I'd get to hang out with her again.

'He's a songwriter you two will really hit it off and you'll never guess what?'

'What?'

'He's been at number one for nearly a month.'

I looked into her beautiful eyes and felt the kick in my stomach, in many ways I didn't need to ask but I had to.

'What's his name?'

'Carl.' She beamed. 'Carl Garl.'

CHAPTER SIXTEEN

On the train journey home I tried to get my head round how Carl could have pulled someone as switched on as Louise. Mind you it hadn't stopped him doing it before, he'd muscled in on my first crush Charlotte and pretty much stole her from me. I remembered it well because the level of deceit around that time had scarred me, emotionally and physically. I looked down at my right hand and opened the palm the white raised scar ran across from left to right then up half my forefinger. It still angered me today to think of how it had happened although it had inadvertently given me a slightly unique guitar stroke because my third finger was never the same after the stitches.

I guess that the rivalry, if you could call it that had started when we were small kids. A neighbour had given me some of his son's old toys so I took them across to Carl so that we could share them out and we set a big blanket out in the garden. Carl went for all the best ones, if there were two moon buggies and one had a broken wheel then I'd be left with that one, if there were two Action Men figures and one had a missing hand then I'd have that one. I got to keep a few extra toys but they weren't very good. Carl said that was the balance and when I tried to take some of the toys back he pushed me over and locked himself in his garage with the best toys.

When we were twelve the same sort of incident happened in the woods one afternoon when I'd found a sheath knife in the mud and he caught me. He ran over and asked to look at it, I was brushing the dirt off and realised it was a really nice one with a carved handle. As the others caught up and started to admire my find Carl pretended to be relieved.

'Aw this is one I lost ages ago.' He said, snatching it away.

'Thanks mate.'

'No it isn't.' I said and tried to grab it back.

'*Is.*' He said, pushing me away.

I got mad and went after it again, I knew what he was doing but he held it too high for me to reach. I jumped around and then dug him in the side with my fist, he dropped his guard but as I took the knife he snatched it away and the blade slit my hand open. We looked down at it in horror as it turned from a thin white slice to a bloodied mess.

I screamed and ran towards the gardens but when I reached the gates I couldn't open them. The others were way behind me and I fainted. When I woke up Bilbo was barking like mad and I was being carried to my parents by Carl's dad Derek. The hospital doctors stitched it up and gave me a tetanus in my bum which really hurt, I'd had a scar on my hand ever since.

Despite all this Carl always insisted it was *his* knife but I knew the truth and so did the gang. It was something that would be repeated over the years in different ways but always the same theme; one of us wanted something so Carl had to have it. It wasn't just me and some people might wonder how you could stay friends with someone like that but he did good things too like letting us play on his snooker table and swingball and he stuck up for me at school if I was getting bullied.

Apart from my scar there were two things that I had never forgiven him for, the first was pushing my brother the day he died and the second was Charlotte. Maybe what he did to Adam could be somehow excused by sheer panic, fight or flight although I struggled with that, Charlotte on the other hand was a deliberate removal of something I cared for deeply.

In Ninety Seventy-Nine, a few months after the knife incident I took her to my first music concert. I remember looking over Carl's shoulder at her and her friend. Charlotte was a huge Blondie fan and I'd used that to try to get her to come with me by getting hold of tickets. Even so I was amazed when she agreed and she'd brought her friend along too so I hoped Carl would pair off conveniently with her.

'Carl, I really like Charlotte, can you distract her friend?' I said as we were rushing up to the front to get the best view possible.

'I think she prefers me.' He said pulling me out the way.

'You can't steal her.'

'She's not yours Davy, she just came to see the band.'

Charlotte had sidetracked to get a T-shirt and I walked back to find her. She appeared with a programme and she'd slipped the new clothing on over her top.

'Hey. It looks really good on you.'

'Thanks.'

With her long hair and big bright eyes I thought that she was an angel, certainly too good for Carl even if she wouldn't date me I thought she deserved better.

'Come on, let's go and find your friend.' She said.

'I think it's a better view here.' I didn't want to be near Carl, I was happy with Charlotte.

'Oh, Okay.' She smiled, shrugging. 'So you think the shirt looks good?'

I nodded with a stupid grin on my face and she gave me a peck on the cheek.

The more people that came in the more pushed together we were until I could feel her pressed up next to me. Her friend found us but luckily Carl was lost in the huge crowd and once the band came on it was impossible to move anyway as it swelled and moved and several times

Charlotte would yelp and hold onto me to steady herself. I didn't think anyone could have taken my eyes off Debbie Harry especially when she was ten feet in front of me but all I could see was Charlotte.

After the gig we headed to a burger place, it did the best hot chocolate I had ever tasted and I kept looking at the gig program and at Charlotte as she spooned the cream off the top of her drink. She noticed my hand where Carl had injured it and ran her finger across it. This made Carl really jealous but her friend was in the way and every time he tried to chat Charlotte up her friend would drape herself over him. I liked her loads for doing that.

We got the train back and left the girls at the station before ours. She kissed me on the cheek goodbye, Carl went to get a kiss but the doors closed. I wondered if she'd be as friendly when we were back at school the next week did the peck on the cheek mean anything? My face still tingled whenever I thought of it and I tried to recall every split second over and over again to keep in my memory forever. It was dangerous, loving someone, caring, they could be taken away from you and leave an imposiible void, I knew that from losing my brother. I had avoided getting close to anyone since the accident but I thought Charlotte was worth the risk.

'What are you smiling about?' Asked Carl as we walked into the Close.

'I think she likes me Carl.'

'No, she was playing cool with me.'

'Don't you dare try and steal her.'

Carl just looked at me and I knew that I'd need to watch out. People aren't always obviously good or bad, they're sometimes a bit of both depending on different circumstances and that's where it gets complicated.

Following on from the concert I'd maintained a close friendship with Charlotte giving her clippings from *Smash Hits* magazines whenever Blondie appeared in them. I was too shy when we were at school to ask so it was easier to steer something from a distance with the help of the new trend, CB radio. I could just about speak to her across the airwaves a quarter of a mile away. She couldn't see me shaking and fumbling for words when we spoke on there and I could write topics of conversation down on a pad ready in case I dried up.

Problems started on the day before we finally set a date to meet up at the weekend. I was just about getting through with my signal when Carl began to talk over me with his bigger aerial - *go figure that Freud.* I'd been setting a time for the meeting with Charlotte and he started trying to flirt with her but she was still interested in seeing me so eventually we confirmed where and when.

Carl who had overheard all this was there on his bike *'by coincidence'.* As we were chatting, eating ice cream in town and wondering where to go he appeared across the road.

'Hey isn't that your friend Carl?' Said Charlotte, suddenly seeming quite excited and squeaky voiced.

'No, I don't think so.'

'Yes it is.' She checked her hair in a shop window and then he rode over.

'Hey, what a surprise.'

I just stared at him and wouldn't say anything, I knew him too well and what he was doing. He wouldn't leave us alone, Charlotte seemed to be giggling at his pathetic jokes and behaving strangely and the more the afternoon went on the more she began to walk closer to him. I didn't think she liked him and had never made much fuss about him but he literally wooed her, in front of me, her date. By four o'clock they were play fighting in the park and by five she was on the back of his bike cycling off to her house.

I walked home alone wondering how both of them could be so rotten towards me. What had I done wrong?

It had made things difficult after that. I'd wanted to speak to Charlotte but whenever she was around especially with Carl I would just blank her or mumble. Maybe if I'd been cooler about the whole thing we could have at least hung onto our friendship, instead Carl dated her for a year then broke her heart and dumped her. This could have been a second chance for me to try and ask her out but Carl wanted to take that away from me as soon as it surfaced.

This time I had the element of surprise on my side. He had always been one step ahead when we were young but now it was my turn.

CHAPTER SEVENTEEN

Even as a widely travelled middle aged man in my forties my mum still managed to make me feel like a kid who'd been out too late. I was standing in the hallway having just walked back in from my long night in the city.

'What happened to you for goodness sake?'

'Don't fret.'

'I thought you'd run off again.'

'You won't get rid of me that quick this time.'

She gave me a look like she'd heard it before and busied herself with some cleaning. She did that when she was stressed, even if the place were spotless she would scrub the same spot on the kitchen top.

I followed her into the kitchen and put the phone on the table.

'Is there a charger for this?'

She pointed to the 'man drawer' that my dad used to keep his stuff in. I recognised some of the screwdrivers and an old spirit level.

'Blimey, didn't he take all this?'

'I think he took two suitcases to Canada and started fresh.'

'Travelling light. Just like me eh?'

'No matter how light you travel you pack up your problems and take them with you Davy. It's not about possessions it's about...' Her voice began to shake.

'You miss him?'

'We were together for years since I was a teenager of course I miss him but that doesn't change anything.'

'So you never been in love since?'

She picked up some bottles of sauce from the table and wiped underneath them, avoiding the question. 'I thought

I did love Stuart but it was never like your father and me, we went back to our teens together. Still, the past is done you can't go back or change it or bring people back, now get yourself up them stairs you smell awful. You remember how to use a bath don't you?'

I found a charger that looked like the right one for Stu's phone and started to walk out, stopping at the bottom of the stairs. I could see mum fighting back tears as she stared out into the garden towards the woods.

'Your dad used to say he could see things in those woods. I never could.'

'What sort of things?'

'He used to tell me that if I couldn't see them then they didn't exist so why bother me with it.'

'Did you ever work out what it was?'

She turned and looked at me shaking her head slowly then she forced a smile.

'Go and get in the bath, it's just me being daft. Oh and Loz phoned earlier by the way, something about finding people on the internet.'

* * *

I soaked in the bath for about an hour and shaved as I wanted to look really good for the evening. I was going back to the city to a party with Louise *and* Carl. I was supposed to text her when I got there and she was going to come down and let me in, then we could surprise Carl. *Hell* was I going to surprise Carl.

I just had enough time to clean up, charge the phone, borrow some clothes from Loz and get back into the city in time for Carl's super bash celebrating our hit record.

Loz told me that he thought he was closer to tracing Carl

on a networking site but I told him I had gone one better after bumping into Louise.

I started to wonder how much I had earned in royalties and imagined the look on Carl's face, as he had to divvy it up with me, fairly this time, half and half, equal for once. If only I could find the old tape that we'd made in the garage it would be concrete, straightforward.

* * *

The city bound evening train pulled away and soon took me through the tunnel that we used to hide in. I pressed my face up against the glass looking for the cubbyholes but it was so dark that I couldn't make anything out. I wondered if we really could have seen people's faces as the trains tore through there at the speeds they got to, whether Kane and his antics had been in my mind, seeing Adam appear like some zombie from a halfway world. Over the years I'd come to many conclusions about it but now I was back it was as if something was over my shoulder again, just out of reach like it had been when I was growing up.

I felt pretty good in Loz's brogues, Ben Sherman shirt and Levis with his three quarter length coat. He had good taste for a recluse and didn't need the togs so why not make use of them, as we were a similar gait? We'd all been through fashion phases in the late seventies and eighties but he'd kept up the Mod style even when the rest of us changed and moved to other things, he liked the order and neatness and my dad was always encouraging him being a Mod the first time round showing him pictures from the sixties. Maybe I'd gone more into the dirty rocker scene as a rebellious thing, none of us want to be like our parents when we're teenagers.

I made my way to the theatre that Louise had written down on the back of her card. The red carpet outside the venue was littered with cameramen and reporters pushing their way into prime positions. I recognised a few 'Z list' faces trickling down the carpet waving and smiling and I would soon be inside there, inside the inner sanctum rubbing shoulders with the smug prats and tapping Carl for the money he owed me.

I sent a text to Louise and waited, watching one of the parading stars being interviewed by a gushing TV presenter. As he walked off she turned to her cameraman.

'What a prick.' She said.

I suddenly thought that perhaps I'd actually been lucky not to get much success over the years, that world could have turned me into one of *them* too, putting on an act all the time, saying the right things to the right people, being in the right place to keep my mug in the press. At least I could wander down to the supermarket in my sloppy clothes and scratch my arse without someone photographing it.

When I was travelling I rarely saw TV but from what I'd seen on television since my return people now wanted to be *famous for being famous* what the hell was that about? Respect for creative output was what counted to me, doing something well, pouring heart and soul into it. A song that moved people, a performance that some kid would remember and go home and start their own band, that was my punk 'do-it-yourself' motivation and fame was a by-product, not the goal. That and getting laid of course.

Another ten minutes passed with no reply to my text and so I decided to call. The phone battery was already down to one bar on the display which was odd as I'd charged it only an hour before. I got Louise's answer phone and figuring that she was probably in a noisy part of the venue I left a quick message. Another ten minutes passed so I tried again, all the time getting a rush of excitement and planning what I would say to Carl. He didn't know what was coming.

'You just wait you smug faced shitbag.' I laughed.

One of the reporters was watching me so I gave her a smile but she just sneered and returned to watching the red carpet. Maybe she'd heard me muttering or I just wasn't who they thought I was at first, sometimes people thought I looked like a famous actor but I guess I just had one of those faces. It had got me a few free meals over the years when I milked it.

After half an hour I was getting fed up waiting and I walked up to the bouncer and asked if there was anyway to get a message to Louise, let her know I was there. I told him my predicament and that she'd probably left her phone in the cloakroom or it was too loud inside. He looked at his clipboard being careful not to tilt it my way, a trick I'd learned in the clubs was to look at the list and point to a random name.

'She's not on the list.'

'Carl Garl's girlfriend not on the list?' I snorted.

'Well I can't help.' He said, winking at a girl by the red rope barrier. She stooped under it and he slapped her bum.

'You owe me for this one.' He whispered to her.

'Right, so because I haven't got tits you are keeping me here. Let me speak to someone else then mate?'

He was distracted again by another 'star' and as I tried to get his attention by grabbing his arm he pushed me in the face. Some of the camera people laughed and jostled and I began to get angry.

'Look I'm sorry.' I shouted, 'it's been a long day and Louise was supposed to meet me here, it's a big surprise for Carl, we're old friends. Seriously, how else would I know that he has a birthmark that looks like a bird dropping on his shoulder?'

'Yeah what magazine did you get that from?' Laughed one of the cameramen, with his super zoom up my nose.

I wished I'd dug out a picture of us all that would have worked, the Polaroid picture of us by the tunnel.

I glanced just inside the doors and there she was, I could see Louise chatting with someone, looking gorgeous as ever. I leant round and shouted to her but there were too many people for her to hear me. I started to step over the rope.

'Where the bloody hell are you going?' Said the bouncer, pushing me back.

'Come on, that's her can you just grab that woman in the blue dress?' I pointed towards her but another bouncer stepped in.

'We'll ask you once more sir, my colleague has told you that you aren't coming in so I suggest you walk away.

'Arseholes.' I yelled but before they could react I held my hands up and hopped back over the rope, as I didn't want a repeat of the security guard incident at Carl's office.

I circled the block for a bit, tried Louise again, Stu's old phone lit up, the battery bar was now flashing but it was working just, after three rings I finally heard a voice struggling to be heard over the din at the other end.

'Hello?'

'Louise?' I shouted.

There was a garbled tinny clang. 'Hello. Who is this?' As I went to speak the phone gave out a long farting noise again and cut me off.

CHAPTER EIGHTEEN

I was surprised how robust a phone could be as I'd stamped on it, kicked it, lobbed it onto some guttering where it bounced back in an arc, off a wheelie bin onto the alleyway floor that ran between the venue and an office block on the other side. I went to pick it up and noticed that there was a fire escape at the back of the building. The only thing I had to get past was a wire fence and that was easy with a transit van parked next to it. I was a bit too sure of myself however as I edged myself down on the other side, catching Loz's Levis and bouncing momentarily like a pair of pants on a washing line before falling down into a puddle.

Dirtied but determined I walked through the private car park and went round the back entrance which wasn't open but I knew from hanging around venues waiting for sound checks that it would only be a matter of time before someone came out for a cigarette. Sure enough after five minutes I heard the welcome click of the fire release door bar inside and the doors swung open. A woman appeared, lit up a cigarette as I approached from the darkness into the new light coming from inside.

'Evening, have you seen Carl or Louise in there?'

She looked me up and down suspiciously, at the muddied trousers and exhaled from her cigarette.

'Who?'

'The guy who's party you're at?'

'Oh right. I think he's in the VIP lounge.'

'Of course, where else would such a talent be' I said pedantically as I stepped inside. 'I'll go have a look then.'

There was a stairwell leading up two flights to a corridor. A double doorway led into a nightclub arena with thumping music and crowds milling around, security men, stars, wannabes and hangers on. It was dark enough to hide my ruffled attire and I blended in grabbing two champagne flutes off a passing tray.

'Excuse me Sir.' Came a voice behind me before I could take a sniff of the drink. Thinking I'd been rumbled already I turned expecting a bouncer but it was a waiter with a tray of fancy nibbles.

'Would you care for anything?'

'That would be super. Cheers.' I said, draining the second champagne and plopping it onto his tray. I took what looked like satay chicken and dipped it in a sauce on the side.

'Amazing.' I said, grabbing two more as he walked off. 'Compliments to the Chef.' I was starting to enjoy myself and meandered around, making small talk and nodding at some of the women, looking for Carl or Louise. I noticed another champagne lady coming past and I took another two glasses, draining one immediately and depositing my skewers onto her tray. As she tutted I snatched another glass and winked. She didn't look impressed but of course I was a guest, possibly a very important one so she had to be very nice about it.

I made my way to a bridge that ran across the dance floor, you could see quite a bit of the club, the stage with a painting of Carl's face, round and smug. It looked like he was going to perform a few songs. After a few minutes a woman in a black dress sidled up to me. I recognised her from outside, the smoker.

'Staring at the tits?' She said.

I looked back down at the painting of Carl. 'You could say that.' I smiled and went to walk off.

'Don't leave me here.'

'Well I'm looking for someone, so if you'll excuse me.'

'And who are you?' She said.

'Davy.'

'And what does Davy do?'

'I write and perform songs in fact I used to do it with Carl.' I left out the bit about playing in shit bars and living hand to mouth in seedy resorts.

She rolled her eyes. 'Whoopee-doo, everyone's a star around here.'

'I wasn't showing off, I just grew up with him that's all. I think he's a dickhead if you must know.'

'I wouldn't know, I only met him tonight.'

'Have you seen him or Louise?'

'I think I could find them for you or at the very least keep you entertained for a while longer. I'm Tanya by the way.'

I shrugged. 'Cool.'

'Tanya will look after you, come on.'

She pulled me by the shirtsleeve and we went across the bridge towards a dimly lit booth. Two men and a woman were already in there, huddled over a table crowded with drinks. One of the men spoke to Tanya and then she was off again, leading me towards the ladies cloakrooms this time. We walked in and she found a free cubicle.

'Erm I thought we were finding Carl and Louise.'

'What's the rush? You've got all night.' She said pushing me into the cubicle.

'I guess Carl can wait a little longer. It's been a while after all.'

'You want something naughty you bad boy?'

I was feeling quite turned on as she rubbed her hands around my shirt and between the buttonholes. It wasn't very nice having sex in a bog, not the sort of thing I'd done since a club in France with a dancer when I was twenty-one.

She took out a silver clip case and sprinkled white powder on top of the basin.

'Oh I thought you meant...'

'I always prefer to screw when I'm high.'

'Oh I see.' I said.

Tanya got a credit card from her clip purse, chopped her own powder into two neat lines and rolled up a fifty-pound note, all the time looking at me and grinning. She bent over and whacked a line up each nostril, 'zoop, zoop' and it was gone. I'd never liked sticking it up my nose, that was where my bogey's grew so I took the other small wrap from her hand and sprinkled it into my champagne. It fizzed and reminded me of a morning after headache pill but this was quite the opposite. I downed my glass and also drank the one she'd brought in with her. My head was spinning by now and I was up for some fun.

She set about undoing my trousers and we began to kiss, and I was actually thanking Carl for leading me to this place even though I hated him for so many other things but I hadn't had any action for a few months. As she pulled on my wedding bits I groped her breast and pushed her against the door. I pulled her hair back and bit her neck; she let out a moan and squeezed my groin. I lifted her skirt and wasn't surprised that she didn't have any underwear on.

'Expecting some action tonight?' I said.

'Just get on with it you naughty pixie.' She said biting my lip.

'Pixie?'

'Yes. I'm your Toadstool Mistress.'

'Isn't it *gnomes* who sit on toadstools?' I asked. I'd never been good at role-play, I kept picking up on the details and it killed the mood.

'Shut up and do me with your pumper gun.'

She bit me again on the lip. I thought that she'd made it bleed, as I could taste it in our kiss, there was quite a bit of blood and I pulled away. I wiped my mouth but it wasn't me, it was coming from her nose along with a blob of cocaine.

'You need a handkerchief.' I said.

She kept hold of me.

'Just screw me.'

'Look as much as I'd like to you look like a half-chewed sherbert dip has exploded over your mush and as for *pumper gun*, try calling it something else could you?'

'You arrogant shit.' She said pushing me back into the toilet and forcing me to sit down. She then slapped me round the face and pulled her dress back over her midriff.

'Hey. You're the one who wanted dirty toilet sex.'

She grabbed the back of my head and forced it into her knee as it came forward, my nose exploded and I couldn't see much. I felt around and she bit my finger.

'Ow!'

'You like it rough baby, is that it.' She said, straddling me.

'What?'

'I'm the boss now.' With that she pulled my hair back, slid off me and punched me in the gut. All the Champagne and snacks came up like a jet spraying out onto her, the wall panels and down my own clothes. I heaved and tried to get to my feet, pulling on her arm, she slipped and went crashing to the floor and I looked down at her, sprawled beside the pan.

'Bollocks to this.' I said, 'You need help.'

I opened the cubicle door and came face to face with Louise who looked at me and then down at the woman covered in misery, blood and vomit.

'Shit Davy what have you done?'

'It's not what you think Louise, she made me come in here and started snorting the marching powder then she gets rough and it's not my scene, you know me better than that.'

'No Davy, no I *don't know you* and Carl was right about you.'

'What?'

'No wonder he didn't want to see you.'

'He *knows* I'm here?'

She turned round and started shouting for help. Women looked at me as I tried to explain.

'Louise if Carl is here then go and get him and we'll sort all of this out.'

I pushed past her and ran back out into the club. Down on stage I could hear the ceremonies had started and Carl was playing the opening bars of *The Sleeping Gallows*. A perfect time to make my entrance.

'Oi.' I shouted but the music was too loud. I tried to get over the railing and use some cabling to get down near the stage like Adam Ant in the *Prince Charming* video but as I got halfway over I felt someone slam me on the shoulder.

'Argh me gooleys!' I screamed as the bouncer yanked me back over the railing onto the floor.

People started to look up and notice the commotion including Carl but they couldn't see past the bright lighting rigs. The bouncer having total recall on my face now began to shout something into his walkie-talkie whilst picking me up with one hand. I managed to break free and tried to run past but another blocked my path and tipped his head at me as if to say *'Your move.'*

I took a right turn back into the ladies bogs, slipping on the blood soaked tile floor into Tanya who was stood there like an extra from *Shaun of the Dead*. I ripped her blouse down as I fell and we both went crashing back into a cubicle.

CHAPTER NINETEEN

I was woken by the sound of the jail door opening. My jaw still hurt from the smack by the bouncer and my ribs were sore, those stairs didn't seem as hard on the way up into the venue as they did during my quick descent once they got hold of me. I'd roughly followed the path of my phone, smashed, kicked, spared the gutter but I did get to see the wheelie bin close up. When the Police arrived I was watching the stars and wondering where I was. I didn't win any bonus points either for pinging the officer's radio aerial and saying *'That's an elaborate looking dildo.'*

The Duty Sergeant appeared and told me that I had visitors, leading me to another interview room with a table. I looked up close to the wall, checking to see if it was a one-way mirror like you see on TV. I waved anyway and then rubbed my nose down it and blew a farting noise, I still felt a bit high from the previous nights revelry.

When I turned round my dad was staring at me shaking his head.

'You bloody idiot.'

Before we had time to enjoy an awkward reunion a stocky man in a long raincoat walked in with a case followed by another who had an accent, at first I thought it was American but then I realised it was Canadian. The guy in the raincoat began to do that speech, you know *'I'm cautioning you for blah blah blah...'*, he even mentioned grievous bodily harm but I just kept looking at dad and grinning. It was some sort of wind up it had to be.

'All this for a scuffle in a club?' I tried to get dad to join in on my side.

'You bloody fool.' He said as the man in the raincoat pushed a photograph across the table.

'You recognise this person?'

I looked at the picture but it wasn't ringing any bells. A man lying in a hospital bed, face bloodied tubes out his nose and mouth. Looked like a poor wretch if ever I'd seen one but it was just like looking at a newspaper article to me.

'No. Sorry. Was he at the club last night?'

'Maybe you remember him more like this?'

I was shown a picture of a man holding a drink up to the camera, beside a blonde woman who I recognised from Miko's in Spain. I looked closer and I could see that it was taken there.

'That's Sara. A waitress. No idea about the bloke though.'

'Who's that behind them?'

He pointed to a tiny piece of the picture.

'I dunno.'

'If you want to see the blown up version it's you, on stage that night.'

He pulled out another page from his case and showed it to me. Sure enough there I was on stage, not the most flattering picture ever but I couldn't argue who it was.

'Bloody hell.' I snorted. 'Technology eh?'

'Davy we have witnesses to say that you had an altercation with this man the night this was taken by his mates, the night before you returned to the UK.'

I was still trying to get my head around what was going on, I had thought it was about the night before but maybe they were going to let me off all that if I helped them with something else. I looked again at the picture and this time something clicked. It was the twat who'd got on stage.

'Oh yes. I do recognise him now. Mr Lobster, he was trouble. Not surprised he's got into trouble, nasty bit of work.'

'We want you to make a statement saying where you

went after you left the bar and any witnesses who can account for your whereabouts between then and when you boarded the plane the next afternoon.'

I looked at them in horror.

'You don't think that I did this?'

'We'll need to have you around if this guy wakes up. You are a prime suspect, GBH, probably more like attempted murder do you understand me?'

'If he wakes up?'

'Lets hope he *does* wake up, if he doesn't then you're looking at murder.'

'No, this is all wrong, he really was pushing his luck that night, he probably left there and got into a ruck with the next person he bumped into.'

'According to his friends they took him to get patched up and he sobered up a bit. The last they saw of him was when he went back towards the bar. Seemed like he wanted a word with you.'

'I was asleep on the beach by then I was nowhere near the bar or any other bars.'

'We have statements from several people. The bar owner where you worked *'Miko'* told this chap that you'd most likely be bumming around on the beach.'

'Oh great, he's trying to stitch me up too? You know if he'd hired security I wouldn't have to fend off idiots like that when I'm trying to perform.'

'Happen a lot does it? You having to beat punters up in the line of duty?'

'That's not what I meant.'

The Canadian man stepped forwards and put another picture on the table.

'So now we're going through the album how about this one?' He banged his finger down onto the picture. I inspected it, it was Drew, an old roadie we used on the Canadian tour, the one who had copped off with my girlfriend and sold one of my guitars for drugs.

'Okay I do know this guy, his name is Drew, he was a junkie who used to steal from my old band years ago. What's he done?'

'He isn't *doing* anything now, in fact not for a long time according to the coroner.'

'What happened to him?'

'Pulled out of a river over in Canada near where your dad lives, near where you toured about the time the forensic guys say he died.'

'But...but...'

'Davy you need to co-operate.' Said Dad.

'Is this why you're here?' I said, 'Did you tell them I knew Drew?'

'Davy they were carrying out an investigation and traced me when they interviewed your old band. I told them you'd stayed with me around the time they reckon this guy was...'

'Murdered, that's the word your father is looking for.' Said the Canadian.

'I've got nothing to hide, I don't care.'

'You *don't care* that a guy you knew has just been pulled out of a river and another young man is in hospital with serious injuries and may die?'

'That's not what I said stop bloody twisting things.'

'We're still looking for the body of Drew's girlfriend, I think you knew her too right Davy?'

'I hardly knew him or Lucinda.'

'How did you know we meant Lucinda?'

'Oh for God's sake they were together at the time I last saw them, lucky guess?'

'It seems you have quite a record elsewhere too.' The

British Inspector said.

'What are you talking about?'

'Theft of a vehicle La Rochelle, assault on a club bouncer in Holland. We're waiting for a report from Malaysia too involving a drowning incident we've had a tip off about and of course last night at the club.'

'Malaysia, where did that one come from?'

I knew the answer already, Louise must have suddenly put two and two together and made five after seeing my behaviour at the club. She must have recalled my off-hand comment about Chuck's accident being murder. That was all I needed, why didn't I think before I opened my stupid mouth?

'Care to comment on any of this Davy?'

'It's a set-up, this whole thing is fixed.' I stood up and slammed my fists on the table. I wanted to get out of there, my hangover from the cocktail of drink and drugs was dancing around every fibre and I started to feel suffocated.

'Sit down.' Said the British Inspector.

'I've seen enough TV shows, you need to charge me or let me go.'

'Bloody sit down Davy.' Said Dad.

'Or you'll send me back to my room?'

He shook his head and gave me a look I hadn't seen since he had broken the news to me that Adam was dead.

* * *

I sat back down for another half hour being grilled and then a solicitor appeared, he spoke with us at length and then I had more weak tea and got taken back to a cell. I spent the next forty-eight hours being interviewed about the same things, Drew, Chuck, Lobster face, the list was getting longer and longer and more bizarre but of course they had nothing concrete to arrest me for so they had to let me go.

The incident with Tanya in the club toilets was the only thing they had any witnesses and she had dropped charges for her own reasons.

I was taken out of the cells back through to the reception desk. Dad was standing there next to a life size *Star Wars* Storm Trooper.

'What the bloody hell?'

Whoever it was patted me on the back.

'Who's your friend Dad?'

'I'll explain on the way back.'

We walked out into the car park and I heard someone shouting my name. It was the Canadian Policeman leaning back on a squad car doing a crossword.

'Don't go too far now Davy.'

'You have a safe flight back.' I said.

'Oh no, I'm staying on for a while, solve the puzzle, five across still missing.' He held up the paper. 'Any ideas?'

We reached Dad's hire car and I looked over to see if he was still watching us, he was.

'What's he on about?'

'Ignore it, they're trying to psyche you out son.'

'Dad you believe I'm innocent right?'

'I think we have a lot of catching up to do.' He said. 'Now get in the bloody car and let's get out of this place.'

The Storm Trooper nodded and stuck his gloved thumb up at me.

CHAPTER TWENTY

I clicked through the red LED dials of my CB radio to channel thirty-two.

'Crank yer handle. Over'

'It's Davy. Over'

'No, your *handle*. Over.'

'I've forgotten what it means.'

'Your CB name.'

'Okay, it's the Wookie.'

'Say over.'

'This is the Wookie *over*.'

'Gotcha Wookie, this is *The Trooper*. Over.'

'Loz can't we just talk normally?' I said.

'You wanted to do this not me. Over.' He snapped.

He was right it was me who'd got all nostalgic about CB radios after finding them in the garage and getting Loz to help me set it up. He had got his two-channel handset still and indulged me with a conversation.

His mum was home this time, she was very different, she'd brought us tea and cakes and appeared too be very happy, calm and serene. Loz said it was her medication that had sorted her out but I was waiting for her to drop the smile and get the hairbrush out any minute.

Loz was also the inhabitant of the Storm Trooper outfit, we'd both been big *Star Wars* fans in the seventies hence our CB Radio names. The reason he continued his obsession as an adult wasn't clear at first until he explained that despite suffering from agoraphobia he *could* apparently go out on occasion if he was dressed as his favourite character.

'Did you really do those things they were talking about last week, over?' Loz said.

'Loz, not over the CB, anyone can hear!' I said.

'Well I'll come back in from the garage annex then, over.' He appeared at the door still dressed in the Storm Trooper body armour. He'd only been a few feet away we might as well have been shouting and saved electricity.

'It's not as much fun as I remembered.' I said, switching off the CB.

'Well there's been mobile phones since, we didn't have anything to compare it to back then really.'

'We spent hours on these things.'

Loz put his handset down and gave me a shifty stare.

'But what they said at the station, was any of it true?'

'What do *you* think?' I said.

'You always were a bit weird.' He said, slurping at a straw that had come from somewhere in the chest plate of his outfit. He'd modified it to carry juice drinks for when he went out. 'I mean after your bump on the head in the woods. Mum said...'

'Yeah?'

'Well I shouldn't repeat it.'

'No come on, let's hear it.'

'She said that you'd gone mental and had a split personality and we should be careful not to challenge you when you spoke about all that hangman stuff in the tunnel.'

'That was sweet of her.' I said.

'Want some of this juice? It's good.'

'No ta. Have you had any luck contacting Carl on the Internet?' I said.

'No. Nothing yet. I sent Charlotte an e-mail.'

'Good.'

'You sure you want to contact her though?'

'Why not?' I said.

'She broke your heart.'

'No. Carl stole her away.'

'The Twins said she preferred Carl and it was all in your head.'

'Oh did they? Well the boys should be here soon and once we track her down we can ask her in person.'

'You know they were married for a while? Had a daughter too.'

'Let's hope she takes after her mum then.'

I had thought about finding Charlotte many times since I'd left Gallows Close all those years ago. It always led me back to feeling betrayed though, her and Carl getting back together the way they did and when I heard from mum they'd got married I decided to try and forget both of them.

'Was Carl just out to stitch me up? I mean what was it that drove him?'

Loz tried to sit back in his outfit and flopped across the sofa. 'He was a bastard to all of us, why do you think I'm like this?'

'What do you mean?' I pressed.

'Well when I went to see a counsellor he did this regression thing, he said sometimes things are triggered in childhood but don't fully manifest themselves til later.'

'So?'

'Turns out that all this started from that cave abseiling weekend with the Cadets.'

'When you broke your ankles?'

'Yep.'

'It was pretty bad but surely that wasn't enough to make you like this?'

'No, there's more. It was Carl who caused it. I never wanted to get him in trouble but when we were in the slate mine he'd tried to scare me, grabbed my rope, that was when I'd panicked and let out too much slack to get away from him, I must have fallen the last twenty feet.'

'Why didn't you say something?'

'I guess I didn't want Carl to hate me for telling on him. Nobody liked tell tales did they?'

'*Tell tales?* Loz the guy nearly killed you.'

He shrugged and tried to catch the straw again slurping at his drink.

The doorbell went, I looked outside to see the Twins pulling faces and sticking their fingers up at me waving beers. Loz went to let them in and I thought about what he'd said about the slate mine. It was really serious and yet Carl had got away with it once again.

Peter broke my train of thought as he walked, complete with his little white oversocks.

'You haven't been banged up yet then?' He handed Loz the booze taking a can off the pack for himself in one swift move.

'No, I'm still out on the loose and a menace to society as you can see.' I said.

'But they said you knew the people?'

'Drew was a thieving junkie, it was inevitable he'd end up like that, Lucinda went from bloke to bloke and is probably living with a rich producer incognito, Chuck was drunk and drowned in a pool I mean Louise told me that before she decided to put me in it. I reckon she thought I deserved to be locked up after the incident at the club.'

'And Lord Lucan, are you clear of that too?'

'Very funny.'

'It's pretty scary isn't it?' Said Ian. 'I mean being accused of murder basically.'

'Well anyone can *accuse* anyone of anything, it doesn't mean it's true and that's what makes Britain so great mate.'

Loz handed the other beers out.

'Well here's to old friends anyway.'

'Murderers, thieves and whores the lot of ya.' Peter said in a mock Pirate voice.

* * *

Ian had some good news on the old tape that I believed held a recording of *The Sleeping Gallows*. There was a time capsule that he'd buried in the wasteland on the missing house plot where Horace's house now stood. He'd asked his mum to dig out his Blue Peter Annual to find the page he'd drawn his 'map' on showing where he'd buried it.

We decided to take a walk over the woods to have a look around the plot, creeping through a gap in the fence to see if Ian might remember roughly where the capsule had been buried.

I thought I could see Horace in the window at one point and we decided to come back later, the last thing I needed was to be caught trespassing.

We headed off up the trail and with Loz lagging behind in his costume I told the twins about the slate mine incident.

'Loz always said it was his own fault.' Ian said.

'I remember Carl nicked a bottle of dad's whisky one night when he stayed over.' Peter said, 'We were about fourteen and I found it just over the fence but I reckon he'd planted it there to collect later.'

'And he tried to get us into fights.' Ian said. 'Just after you left he told me and Peter these two kids from another estate were after us and he'd somehow managed to get word to them something similar about us. When we eventually bumped into them it was about to kick off but it didn't take long too suss that it was a set up.

'What did you do?'

'We all actually became good mates. I think that was

when we stopped listening to the bullshit that came out of Carl's mouth or hanging around with him. Not long after that he moved into the city.'

* * *

We carried on walking up to a huge sea of bluebells, the wide plane verge before the new road crossed the tail. Charlotte and her friends would pick them to make *'perfume'* in jars with water. By the side of a tree we saw a rusty old bin lid.

'I remember we used to use them as shields.' Said Peter.

'And make our own bows and arrows.'

'My kids are too busy on little computer games now.'

'All we had was 'pong' and the early Ataris'.

'ZX81 anybody?'

'Ooh all I had was a brick with a piece of string.'

'String? I had to make do with a piece of dog hair tied to my brick.'

We crossed over into the second section of the woodland towards the trail and the joking stopped. We all knew where my poor brother had gasped his last breath as we passed it, the dead flowers still propped up against the huge oak. It seemed as if it was all for nothing now as I peered back at the link road, the stupid protest did nothing to stop the developers.

The farmer's old fence was beaten down and we hopped over heading down the trail to the railway woods. There was now a ten foot black metal fence.

'Oh well we won't be going any further today.' Ian said.
I walked along the perimeter a bit and saw some earth had been dug away; there were always kids around trying to find ways to break the rules or cross barriers.

'We can squeeze under here.'

'Loz can't in that suit.'

I looked at Loz who shrugged and sat down on a stump, sliding off it onto the grass. We laughed.

'Okay, Loz stay on guard here right?'

He saluted.

The twins and I managed to dig away a bit more earth and slide under the fence at the bottom. We walked across the top of the path and then slid down the embankment grabbing the roots and chalk rock as if we did it every day. I could remember every step, regressing further into my past with each foothold. Ian stopped at the tunnel roof and hesitated, Peter called him a chicken and followed me right down towards the tracks. We jumped the last few feet down onto the gravel and peered into the tunnel entrance, the smell hit me like a tidal wave and took my breath away.

'Bloody hell, I can't believe we used to go in there.'

'Coming to the cubby hole?' I said.

'I'll get Ian.' Peter started to climb back up the chalk siding.

'Come on Ian.'

'No, if we go in there I want Loz and Carl here too. The whole bunch of us, we have to do it together.'

'You're just being chicken.' Peter said, breaking into a verse of *Fear Of The Dark*, by Iron Maiden.

'Oh give over Pete, let's get back.' Ian said.

'He sounds like he's had enough for today I'm afraid.'

The wind from the tunnel picked up and crept around my neck. I peered back inside I knew that there should be a whining on the track if it was a train at the other end approaching but it was quiet apart from the sound of gravel moving inside. I looked deeper into the tunnel and walked a few paces in.

'Hello? Is anyone there?' It was too dark for a workman

they always wore bright orange jackets so I picked up a piece of the rock gravel at my feet just in case.

'Anyone in here?' I said, throwing the rock in a slow arc into the darkness and hearing it land with a clacking sound. I could hear Peter up the side of the embankment and decided to go back out. As I turned I felt something whistle over my head, there was a bump as an object hit the wall to my left.

I thought it was kids messing around but there was nothing but the tiny light at the far end of the tunnel piercing the darkness. I looked down and saw a small shoe lying beside the train track.

I reached down to take a closer look, it was a kids shoe, a *'Clark's Commando'*, but they hadn't made them since the seventies. Since I'd lost one being chased by workmen.

CHAPTER TWENTY-ONE

I ran into the tunnel, trying to find whoever it was inside there who might have thrown the shoe. Was it a sick joke? I wouldn't have put it past Carl to set something like that up, maybe the others were in on it too?

I passed a cubbyhole and checked it but there was nothing, then a second one on the other side, a third and before I knew it I was quite deep inside the tunnel consuming me more with each step.

As I reached the sixth cubbyhole I saw a flash of light at the other end and a whining on the track. I knew it was a train and stepped deep into the cubbyhole until it passed me. I waited, peering out as the white headlight grew closer reflecting off the nearside wall and then I knew I would see the flash of the yellow engine zoom past me soon.

I closed my eyes, feeling the metallic wind as it got to my face, I was back in time, back in my childhood and the feelings and sensations were the same.

I was so busy concentrating on the train at the far end of the tunnel that the second one on the far side track took me by surprise hurtling in from behind me and that was when the wailing began. I could feel the air being forced through the tunnel and I suddenly realised it was the pressure being forced through the chimney grills, it wasn't a ghost boy at all, it was science, it was wind through a grill like a gigantic whistle.

Feeling proud of myself for working it out I waited for the noise to drop as the trains passed and opened my eyes. My eureka moment was shattered by the motionless train just feet in front of me on the track. I looked up into the carriage to see Kane, waving at me with his other hand on the emergency chord wrapped around his wrist.

The bang of a side door echoed around the tunnel and I looked to see a figure stepping down onto the gravel. Twisted and bent like I'd seen over thirty years before was Adam, my brother. This time he had company too, the growling Bilbo as he jumped down beside him.

I stepped out onto the gravel and walked towards them slowly, Bilbo whining and scratching at the ground. There was some light coming into the tunnel from the carriage windows and as I got closer I could see he was dirty, a matted coat not like the shiny healthy mane he used to have. He limped too and I remembered that mum had told me he'd been hit by a car and spent the last few years of his life with a dodgy leg.

Adam got back up onto the train and then whistled to Bilbo. I walked alongside the track and boarded the carriage as it began to move off, jumping up instinctively as I had done in my childhood.

The door closed and the train began to move back into the tunnel towards the other end from where it had appeared. The heavy metal rhythmic clacking of the wheels beat over the tracks rocking the train, the lights inside the carriage flickered and when they grew dim the sparks from the wheels outside flashed against the fogged windows.

It was raining hard, the dusk forming a grey slate blanket over the platform as we stopped. I followed Kane, Adam and Bilbo off the train and down the trail in silence. I knew we were headed into the town and toward the main courtyard; the one Kane had shown me decades before.

We reached the well, you could hear drops of heavy rain as they hit the bottom a hundred feet down inside. We walked up the alleyway past the jail and the inn which was empty, towards the Gallows courtyard.

There was a creaking noise, two undertakers were taking a body down and laying it on a cart beside the platform and covering it over with a large dirty blanket.

Kane and Adam stood beside the cart and waited for me as Bilbo trotted along bobbing with his bad leg, stinking of old rainwater and growling at me. As I approached the cart Kane beckoned me to come as close as I could.

'Welcome back Davy, it's been like the twinkling of an eye but I have missed you.'

'I don't understand, why am I back here?'

'Because you *should* be, you came back to face it, how else are you going to get justice?'

'Justice?'

He pulled the dirty matting back from the body to reveal a face, purple blue, the neck red raw from the gallows. I recognised it at once. Carl.

'If you dig up the past you're going to get dirty.'

I saw the body twitch, Carl sat up and hit me with the back of his hand, it felt like a mallet and I went flying back into the mud.

'You should have stayed away Davy.'

'Don't listen, fight him.' Shouted Kane.

'This isn't real.' I looked up and Adam had vanished.

'Well you won't mind me doing this then?' Carl said.

He slid off the cart and pulled out a long pitch fork from the side rail. He walked over towards the gallows and from the back steps of the platform Adam appeared, this time he was how I remembered him, playing with a small Airfix kit model and oblivious to Carl approaching.

'You can't save him this time either.' Carl said as he raised the pitchfork.

I had to do something and scrambled to my feet, running

across the mud as fast as I could yelling for Adam to lookout. I reached the platform but when I got to the top of the steps Carl and Adam were gone. I turned to see Kane watching me.

'He's gone.'

'Oh no he hasn't.'

He yelled back like he was at a pantomime.

'Just tell me what's happening.'

Kane blew his cheeks out and threw his arms down.

'I tried to warn you.'

I felt a thump in the middle of my back, a heavy boot sent me hurtling over the edge of the platform to the mudded courtyard. Carl jumped down beside me and lunged with the spiked end of the pitchfork, I rolled out the way and kicked out as hard as I could, it made contact but it felt like I was hitting a tree trunk.

I stood up and ran at him, he swatted me away and I slammed into the side of the gallows platform collapsing and winded, fighting for breath. I could hear noises from inside now, scraping on the wood. I lay sprawled on the ground looking up at the sky, it was swirling and lightning cracked through it in thick wide bolts.

Adam appeared over the top of the platform, sliding on his belly, looking down at me, his head kinked and bloodied. He reached out with his limp pale hand. I scrambled to my feet and began to run towards the alleyway and the main courtyard, if I could get there I could reach the path back to the station.

'Get him Bilbo.' Carl yelled, the dog hopping along and barking at my heels despite its injury. I got up and began to run but I couldn't shake him. Carl was now gaining on me as I reached the alleyway between the jail and the inn. He started wailing louder and louder until it sounded like the ghost boy from the tunnel chimneys.

'It's just the wind hitting the grill.' A voice from one of the inn windows shouted.

'Two trains passing together.' Another voice, this time from the jail bars, I span round and tried to see their faces getting too close and they grabbed me, I kept saying to myself that it was all in my head, this wasn't real, but the grip on my arm felt like ten inch nails were slowly puncturing my flesh. As I tried to break free I could feel the mud slip under my feet, I could smell the dirty sewage in the old streets. Dreams were never this real.

A crowd appeared at the end of the alleyway and surrounded me. One of them, a large man yanked me away from the grip of the jail inmate and pushed me to the floor.

'I told you to get a job ya bum.' He said.

'Do I know you?' I stammered.

'Another scotch Davy?' Said another of the mob.

Three or four of the crowd grabbed me by my limbs and carried me back up the alleyway towards the gallows. I looked up at the sky wild with an electrical storm, lightning flashes piercing the void and thunder shaking the whole town to the beat of the mobs footsteps.

A young boy ran alongside me, he had a long stick with pieces of string hanging off it and some puppets. He waved them at me, five little rag dolls but they weren't strung up like marionettes by their arms and tops of the head, they were strung up by their tiny cotton necks like criminals.

'Let me go.' I screamed out as a flash of lightning struck the ground forcing them to drop me onto the alleyway floor which was cold and hard and I blacked out.

* * *

I came round again and felt one of them wrestling with me, I pushed them away but they wouldn't let go.

'For God's sake Davy.'

I realised my eyes were still shut tight and opened them to see Peter staring at me, pressing me against the wall of the train tunnel.

A train was hurtling past but we weren't in a cubbyhole and the train was dangerously close. When it finally passed I threw up across the track and fell over on the gravel. Ian appeared from a cubbyhole further along the tunnel. We were about a third of the way in, I'd ran much further than I remembered, we were almost underneath Horace's plot; I could see the light shining down from the grill in the chimney.

'What happened?' I said.

'You disappeared back into the tunnel.'

'Did you see anyone chasing me?'

'No all we could hear was you shouting and screaming. You nearly ran in front of that train.'

'You never saw anyone else?' I looked around frantically, scared that any moment I could be back there.

'No. Just you, Ian and me. Come on, we need to get you home.' He said as they took an arm each and began carrying me back out of the tunnel.

CHAPTER TWENTY-TWO

Charlotte had replied to Loz's e-mail enthusiastically and invited us over to see her. By the look of Charlotte's street it didn't seem like she was living the lifestyle of an ex-wife to a hit songmaker.

A group of youths hanging around started to walk over as soon as we pulled up outside.

'You sure this is it?' Peter said.

'Yeah. Sat Nav says it's right here.'

The group of youths eyed us up and down as we got out, a tall lad in a grey hoody piped up first.

'What's with the robot?' He said, pointing to Loz who was trying to get out the car but the child lock was on.

I went round and opened the back door for him.

'He's harmless, unless you're part of the Rebel Alliance?'

I don't think he got the joke. There was some mumbling and posturing but it didn't phase me, not after travelling through some of the cities I'd stayed in during my travels. I'd seen street kids in Rio younger than these with a look in their eyes that made you pity and fear them at the same time. At least they had a reason to be pissed off, they never had computer games or a roof over their heads they just had the rags on their backs.

I lent on the car, folding my arms and looking at the group, wondering what the pecking order was. I knew that we'd been that age once and up to mischief but there seemed to be a resignation among some of them now, belying the fact they were at the dawn of their lives and could do so much more. Technology had advanced more than you could imagine since the seventies with computers the size of a house but it had left community programmes long behind.

Peter walked up to the grey hoody and pointed over to me, whispering something to him. The youth looked at me, then at his friends and his demeanour changed as they began to slope off.

'What did you say to him?'

'I told him that you were out on bail for serious crimes including murder and that you were itching for an excuse to justify the sentence you're about to be given. Nothing worse than a man with zero to lose right?'

'Great. Thanks a lot.' I said.

There was a fridge in the garden and two upturned bikes rusting against the fence. The doorbell played a fuzzy tone version of a Christmas carol as we waited and then the door bolts pinged and rattled, the door finally opening.

'Hello boys!' Came the sweet voice from that broad smile and my stomach kicked and I realised just how nervous I was even twenty-five years later. 'What the heck is that?' She pointed at the white suited figure.

'Our personal *Robocop*? It's a long story.'

She shook her head and laughed.

'Still the same bunch of idiots I see, come in.'

We filed through the narrow hallway into a small front room with a kitchenette at the back. It was tiny for living quarters but clean. As Charlotte made tea the Twins told her about their kids and she in turn pointed to pictures of her own daughter, now in her mid-twenties and at university.

I picked one up and noticed the resemblance to her, she reminded me of Charlotte when I'd last seen her although she hadn't aged much herself, some people seemed to stay beautiful no matter how old they got.

'She wasn't one of those outside then, the welcome committee?'

'Those kids? Oh no. They're pretty harmless though

really, I feel sorry for them there's nowhere to go anymore, I mean we had youth clubs and things to do didn't we?'

'We certainly didn't go around looking for fights and stabbing each other.' Ian said.

I held my hand up showing the scar in my palm. 'Well sometimes some of us got close.'

'You still have that.' Charlotte said, taking it in her hand and running her finger along it. She kissed my cheek and her hair brushed against my face. 'He was a git wasn't he?' She said, closing my hand gently and smiling. 'You were no Angel either though Davy.'

'And how about the father, is he a good guy?'

'Like I said, he was a git.'

'You mean that's Carl's daughter?'

'You wouldn't think so, he's had nothing to do with her since she was a baby.'

* * *

We stepped out the back of the house onto a postage stamp garden patio. I couldn't help but wonder if she was as happy as she looked. I'd noticed some final reminders on the side in the living room but she'd raised a kid and got them into University, she was trying to live like an Adult; I was being accused of murder and still cooped up at my mums' house with no rent money. I think she probably won that one as far as success stories went.

Charlotte filled us in on her brief time with Carl. Their marriage was a sham from the start and it had only lasted a few years. It seemed Charlotte had fallen in love with him but the only person Carl loved was the mirror, in more ways than one. Charlotte had got him his first big break; an introduction to a music producer who she worked for, Carl began to write songs for various 'production line' bands. When Charlotte was pregnant Carl was out drinking, doing drugs and trying to emulate what he thought rock stars did.

It was during a song writing trip to the Bahamas that they married on a beach but Carl never filed the papers when they got back so when she finally tried to divorce it wasn't as hard as she had thought, never being recognised on British soil.

Due to the mix up with the marriage Charlotte had not been able to get as much money in the split and Carl had her thrown out of the huge house while telling the court that their daughter wasn't his.

Loz mumbled through the gap in his helmet mouthpiece.

'Can't you take that off here?' Charlotte said.

Loz lifted it off, looking around like a spaceman testing the atmosphere on a new planet as if any moment his head would implode. He smiled then plopped it back on.

'Sorry, maybe inside I can but it's still a bit freaky.'

'Did you know that Davy's on the run?' Said Peter.

I reached to punch him but he got out the way. Now I was going to have to go through it all again with Charlotte so I sent the lads back inside to make more tea while I explained. She sat there and listened quietly and although it was very serious all I could think about was how beautiful she looked and how I still had a soft spot for her. I had never been romantic really but when there was a break in the grey skies and the sun broke through the clouds onto her it made me feel as if I was sitting with an ethereal being.

I finished my tale and she sat back and blinked slowly, popping her wide eyes at me.

'Davy, I don't quite know what to say.'

'You believe I'm innocent though?'

She nodded.

'That's enough for me. Knowing that you believe me is the most important thing but don't tell the lads they'll get jealous.'

'Really?' She threw her head back and laughed. 'If you felt like that you never would have left without saying goodbye all those years ago.'

'I did leave a letter.'

'I never got it.'

'But I definitely sent it, it had a painful explanation of why I wanted to leave and there were song lyrics in it, I wrote it just for you.' I played with my tea mug.

'I would have remembered.'

I shrugged. It was too late now to worry or change it.

'Anyway you're here now.' She reached over and squeezed my hand.

'So, why are you so interested in finding Carl, do you want to patch things up or is it revenge?'

'At first I thought it was to get back at him but as soon as I got back to the UK I realised it's much more, not just Carl, it's everything. I feel like I've been running all my life but I never figured out what I was running *from* and I think I've started to unearth it.'

'So, what is it?'

I looked away; I didn't know how to explain the things that had started to happen again with Kane, Adam's ghost and the visions. I wanted to tell her everything but I couldn't find the words, how do you explain that you feel as if you're carrying two souls around with you sometimes? I could see Carl sitting there with us, laughing. *'Go on tell her about your mad world Davy, she told me you were creepy … in fact we all used to talk about the men in white coats coming for you one day!'*

'I'll tell you when things come together eh?' I said, shaking the image of his smug face away.

She nodded and lent closer to me.

'I hope you find what you're looking for.'

'Yeah.'

'Davy, do you think you'll stay this time?'

'Seeing you lot again is a kick but it doesn't take long to spot the changes.'

'You mean in us?'

'No, the town, the surroundings as I used to see them in my memory, it's so different. I was walking down the shop the other day, the one dad used to stop off at and get our comics, it's so run down and dirty now. I wanted to remember things as they were. It's like when Adam died, the only thing I could remember for years was the twisted images in my nightmares but eventually as I travelled I remembered him as he *was* doing his model kits and all fresh faced. That's how I wanted to remember this place when I leave.'

'I think you're looking for innocence. Everything changes.'

'Maybe.'

'So where is home for you now?'

'I don't think there's such a place anymore.'

Charlotte sighed. 'This estate was pretty nice when we first moved here years ago but it's a hell hole now. I wish I could get out.'

'Maybe this time I'll take you with me?' I said.

We sat there for a while in a comfortable silence. I wondered how life might have turned out if Carl hadn't got between us, if we'd had a chance. We could have been proud parents happy with the simple things in life in a nice part of the world instead of being in a place I swore I would never return to, digging up old monsters.

And they were closer than I realised.

CHAPTER TWENTY-THREE

We drove up to the gatehouse where Carl lived, Charlotte had told us he was probably still holed up on the private estate she had been unceremoniously evicted from. A security guard came out like some sort of clockwork toy twitching a bit, I suspected he wasn't used to cars like Peter's turning up to such an exclusive estate, it was usually top of the range sports cars or Mercedes people carriers.

'We're looking for our friend Carl who lives here.'

'Okay Sir, what number is it and I'll check with the house?'

'Thirty-five but we wanted to surprise him.'

'Well I can't let you in I'm afraid, not unless you are on my list of expected guests or you let me clear it with the house.'

I rolled my eyes, another *'jobsworth'* was getting in the way of my progress to reach Carl. I had little time.

'If you ain't on the list you ain't coming in?' I said.

Loz giggled inside his outfit and the security guard gave him a stare.

'That's pretty much it.'

'It's a party surprise see, singing Birthday gram?'

'My boss will fire me if I let anyone through these gates who do not meet protocol.'

'Look mate.' I said, stepping out. 'Protocol and me, we just seem to clash so how about if there's a few quid in it for you?'

'I would advise you get back in your car and leave or I will call the Police.' He said, staring right into my eyes.

'Okay, call the bloody house.' I said. 'Ruin the surprise.'

'Right you are Sir.'

We waited as he retreated into his little hut for several minutes. I could see him looking over and nodding now and then. He then hung up the phone and marched back down towards us.

'I'm sorry but there's nobody in at the house, you'll have to make an appointment.'

'Let's go then. Get back in the car Davy.' Said Ian.

'No wait a minute' I said, 'that was a long phone call for someone who wasn't home, I saw your lips moving like a third rate ventriloquist.'

The guard blinked and drew breath; he hadn't expected us to be so persistent.

'I will ask you again Sir, please leave the forecourt.'

I stared back at him, I was sick and tired of this, every time I tried to get to Carl this happened like a platform computer game with levels of *'Bosses'* at the end but eventually I had to get to him somehow.

'I am going to give you one more chance to be a good chap and let us through, if not I am going to drive this car through the barrier.'

'What?' Said Peter out the window.

'That's right, we'll ram it and charge your bosses for obstructing a legitimate guest of a resident.'

'Will we?' Peter said.

'Ten seconds.' Said the guard.

'Okay. Ten seconds it is.' I agreed.

He looked at his watch and I asked Peter to step out of the car, winking at him.

'Five seconds.' Said the guard.

I sat in Peter's estate car and revved the engine as he watched and mouthed to me what would happen if I wasn't just having a laugh.

'Two.'

I revved it again and put it into gear.

'One.'

I yelled out and put my foot to the floor, the engine

raced, Loz and Ian screamed out then the car went bang and stalled. Loz flew forwards and head butted me with his Storm Trooper helmet. The guard lent in, grabbed the keys and was yelling about the fact he'd already hit the panic button in his little hut and there would be Police coming soon.

I reached out of the window and grabbed his coat, holding onto it and tearing it. He didn't like that, pulling out a telescopic nightstick and getting me in a headlock. Loz got out and started wrestling the guard but he couldn't move much in his outfit so it was pretty ineffective. God knows how Darth Vader ran an army of them and raged war with that gear.

Ian just sat in the back seat saying how much he had liked his life before I'd come back.

As all of this was taking place a Ferrari came out of the exit twenty feet away across the forecourt. The driver looked over at the commotion and as I caught his gaze in between getting my breath I knew who it was. The number plate confirmed my suspicions. 'CRL G8RL'.

'There he is.' I hissed, fighting for air.

The Ferrari's tyres squealed and it raced off up the lane.

'You said he wasn't in.'

'He doesn't want to see you now calm down.' Said the guard.

I decided to do the only thing I could and that was to bite the guard's arm forcing him to drop the keys on the floor. Loz barged him out the way.

'Get the bloody keys Peter.' I yelled out.

He flicked them over to me; I stuck them back into the ignition and got the car going. Reversing it in the entrance I flung the passenger door open and Peter jumped in. Loz was running around in his outfit waving his arms and trying to get back in the other rear door. Ian helped him onto the seat as we raced after Carl.

We got to the end of the lane which filtered onto a dual carriageway, there was no way we were going to catch a car like Carl's but Peter said there were some roadwork's on the one-way system ahead which would slow him down. All the time Ian was babbling and fretting about being caught and sent to jail and Liz finding out, I told him that it was *me* who needed to worry with the things I was being accused of they were looking for excuses to bang me up.

By the time we hit the road works the traffic was getting thicker and moving into one lane. We could see a gap in the cars ahead and every now and then the low Ferrari bonnet would sneak into view as it tried to get past someone but we were all only going one way like grain down a funnel.

We were going about ten miles per hour as we merged into one lane and I began to strife for position in front of the car to our right. They beeped their horn and I looked at the man driving and his wife. I leant out and shouted over.

'Police business sorry about that but we're chasing a right scum bag.'

'Ooh how exciting.' Said the wife winding her window down. 'They're having a bit of a chase Roger.'

'He needs to learn to indicate.' Muttered the husband.

'Oh you're no fun anymore, let him in front.'

He rolled his eyes and waved me in so I thanked the lady.

'Ian can you see a clear run down the other side of the bollards?'

Ian peered down and saw that there was about a hundred feet before a digger truck. He relayed this to me and I thanked him before swinging left and across one of the orange bollards that banged on the underneath of the car.

'You stupid shit Davy.' Yelled Peter as I accelerated alongside onlookers as far as I could, veering back into the queue before the truck and squeezing in two vehicles behind Carl's Ferrari. The van in front had seen my manoeuvre in his mirror and began to shout something out at me.

'Sorry Peter but you did stack my bike with the cow horn handlebars once.'

We carried on for several hundred yards and then I could see there was a turn ahead as the road works ended and it went back into two lanes. Carl would be getting away if I didn't do something quick.

'I just had an idea. Please forgive me Pete.'
I whacked the car into second gear, accelerating hard into the back of the van. You could hear a second crash. If my calculations were right it would be Carl's Ferrari.

The van man jumped out too so I dodged round the back and along the other side.

'Calm down mate it's all insured.' I shouted in a *Michael Winner* voice at the van driver. Cars were sounding their horns and drivers were getting out. Carl had staggered out of his driving seat and was looking very upset I'd never seen him like that ever, he started heaving and puked all over the front of the van.

'This is an insurance nightmare, you better give us your details mate.' Said the Van Driver.

'Piss off.' Carl wiped the spit from his chin.

'Don't have a go at me, it was this clown's fault.' He said, thumbing over to me.

'Fancy bumping into you Carl, I think we need to talk.' I said.

Carl strode towards me, his eyes clouded over, I thought he was going in for a hug but he punched me feebly and then collapsed making weird noises as he shook on the floor.

CHAPTER TWENTY-FOUR

Carl was safely tucked away in hospital, the reason he had collapsed after dealing me a cheeky punch was that he had experienced a seizure brought on from cocaine that had been cut with something usually used to soften hard water in washing machines. The Police and Ambulance had turned up and while arranging for his car to be towed the officers found an open wrap of powder on the car seat. The Police told me that we'd done the public a favour as he could have crashed into anyone in that state and hurt them instead of a small shunt in the middle of road works. The van driver didn't agree with him on this as he exchanged insurance details with Peter and they both looked close to killing me.

We had to wait until Carl got out of Hospital before we could get in touch again to try and arrange a meeting but by the middle of the following week the twins' mum had found a *Blue Peter* annual in the loft, something I needed to get hold of to find the time capsule and the tape so I could prove to Carl I had written the song with him. Ian had flicked through the annual to find his old notes about hiding the time capsule. The problem was that it wasn't *his* annual it was Peters, the twins had identical presents when they were growing up and the only copy was the wrong one.

We decided to have another look anyway as it was towards the back of the plot where Horace now lived near the tunnel chimney, it might jog Ian's memory if we could get in again without worrying we were being watched. It was always in the back of my mind to ask Horace's permission to do this but there was something in my instinct that held me back. His link to the land was still puzzling me.

He liked to go out for drives in the Crossley so all I needed to do was get them over when Horace went out so I kept a watch on his drive and tried to work out any patterns in his movements. I didn't want to ask Mum or involve her too much besides Dad was staying there for a while since the whole Police situation had kicked off. He was being very quiet about his thoughts on the matter and of his ex-wifes new 'companion'.

One evening I went out and sat at the front of our path on the gatepost, drinking coffee and watching the world go by. Oliver and his sister were on their bikes doing circuits of the Close. Horace's car was in the drive and I could feel there was someone at the window just out of my eye line, I turned round and there he was looking out although he never waved or acknowledged me, he just kept staring into the Close and puffing at his pipe blowing thin plumes of smoke.

'You see him watching?' Came a little voice.

I looked back down to see Oliver who had cycled over. 'Is that the man who told you about me?'

Before he answered there was a shrill voice across the close.

'Oliver, come in now, you haven't got any lights on that bike.'

'It's my mum. I have to go.'

'What else has he said to you?'

'I have to go now.'

He looked scared. Oliver pedalled over to his house and I got down off the gatepost and walked towards Horace's, marching up the front path. I banged on the door, rang the bell but there was no answer. I stood back and looked up, he'd gone from the window. I opened the letter box and peered inside to a wide reception hallway, some stairs in the centre and two half-dead yucca plants standing guard at the bottom.

'You're scaring small children now?' I shouted through, the letter box and it echoed around inside. 'I know you're there, what are you up to Horace?'

The door clicked and opened. I stood at the entrance and looked around. There wasn't anyone there but then I heard a cough and glanced up. Horace was at the top of the stairs.

'Come in.' He said, descending the staircase in his highly polished oxford cap shoes.

He blew a plume of smoke towards me.

'I think it's time we had a chat.'

* * *

The house was surprisingly bigger than it looked from the outside, once you got past the entrance hall it opened up on both sides, and round towards the garden, it was sparsely furnished with wooden floor throughout, not the modern laminate version these were hardwood boards that creaked and you felt your feet click and slide along the high polish as you walked.

Horace stood by the window in the back room pouring out two large whiskeys in a stream of dusk light that filtered in from large French windows. His dark brown suit jacket and braces pulled over a crisp white shirt, peg trousers with turn-ups made him look like something from an old photograph or gangster movie. Big band music played from a gramophone, an old contraption that piled records on top of one another with a clunking sound that made the whole unit wobble. The room reminded me of my Nan's house, dimly lit from table lamps, mahogany handmade furniture, occasional rugs and art-deco ornaments. Funny how people clung onto what they were used to really but then again it was superior craftsmanship in those pieces, they were made to last forever not like the modern matchstick bulk furniture that wouldn't last beyond a season or two.

'Ice?' He said.

'You got lager?'

'All out, just the best single malt I'm afraid.'

'Ice then.'

He dropped two cubes into my glass and walked over, handing it to me in a cut crystal tumbler.

'Cheers.' I said, sipping at the hard taste as it hit my lips.

'Please sit down.' He said.

I looked around and found a wooden dining chair beside a cabinet.

'Bit empty isn't it, this place?'

'Maybe you're just used to clutter these days. I find space and tidiness help me think clearly.' He smiled and walked to the gramophone. 'Music is such reliable company don't you think?' He placed his drink on a shelf beside some white pipe cleaners and reached into his pocket for some fresh tobacco which he patted into his pipe, produced a brass Zippo lighter and lit it almost disappearing in a smokey haze.

'You used to make little toy figures with these.' He said, holding up the pipe cleaners.

'I don't remember.'

'Your mum told me, they were coloured though, blue, red, yellow.'

I suddenly remembered it. A scene with mum at the kitchen table, Adam was doing his homework and I was making little men out of pipe cleaners. I turned their feet so they could stand up.

'I'd forgotten that ever happened.'

'There's a lot of things we forget.' Said Horace pacing over to the patio windows. 'Some of them deliberately, some because they are of no use. We could hardly store our entire lives after all.'

'Thanks for the tit bit. Any more wisdom you want to share with me?'

'No but I have a question.'

'Oh goody it's my turn is it?'

'How is the Police inquiry going Davy?'

'They didn't have anything on me, all rubbish.'

'Not looking good though is it Davy? Time is running out for you.'

'Not at all.'

Horace grinned at me and gave a throaty cough, blowing another smoke cloud.

'You've been lackadaisical in your surveillance work, watching the house for days anxiously. You definitely look like something's up.'

'Well you're wrong.'

'You can borrow a spade if you want, there's a shed up the top by the tunnel chimney, that's where it is right?'

I stopped halfway through a tug on the whisky.

'I don't know what you're talking about.'

'So it wasn't you and your pals the other day nosing around?'

He opened the patio doors, whistling up the garden. I peered over towards him and past into the early evening it was getting dark. I could hear steps, light and quick a bit erratic. Horace moved aside to let the creature in.

'Hello old friend.' He said to the dog as it hobbled in and tilted its head to sniff the room; it padded over to me and stopped.

'Bilbo?'

The dog looked up at me but it wasn't looking at me with the soft eyes I remembered as a kid, it was the dirty mud caked animal from the gallows courtyard and it unsettled me.

'Dug up a tin didn't you boy?' Horace said.

Bilbo barked and a fleck of drool came from its mouth landing on my foot.

'But Carl's dog died years ago.' I said.

'You need to get out Davy, there's still time. Just go anywhere but get away from here.' Horace stepped out onto the patio and I followed, wiping my shoe as I passed the floor length curtain.

'The tin had some doodling and memories from a group of kids and so I decided to rebury it.'

'Was there a tape inside?'

'Let me see, a tape. I'm not familiar with the new technology as you can see I am far more at home with the vintage world.'

The dog came out and started sniffing around, Horace reached down and looked at the animal, whispering something out of my earshot and it went hobbling towards the garden again.

'Horace, was there a bloody tape?'

'You don't need the tape Davy, you've got Kane.'

'How do you know about him?' I said.

Horace peered up the garden and watched as Bilbo disappeared into the darkness near the train chimney.

'The same reason you know him Davy.'

'So he's real?'

'As real as you are to me Davy.'

'Why is he back, what does he want?'

'He's never been away, it is you who has come back to dig up the past.'

Horace grabbed my arm, his strong grip a shock for someone so old. His face was close and I could smell that breath again, like the train tunnel, like old rusty metal and soot.

'If you dig up the past you're going to get dirty so leave the time capsule well alone, leave Carl alone and forget about Kane. You need to get out of here before it's too late.'

Bilbo started to bark at something at the end of the garden there was a shout and the sound of wood breaking, it sounded like a fence.

I dropped the glass of whisky, it smashed and I ran into the darkness after the Dog. I knew that I had to find that time capsule and he knew where it was. I reached the far end of the garden and came to some trees and thick thorn bushes near the tunnel chimney. I tried to control my breathing and listen carefully, my heart thumping in my chest.

There was a noise in the bushes by a dilapidated shed.

'Bilbo? Come here there's a good boy.' I edged nearer and pushed a thorn bush to one side where I thought the animal was hiding between it and the shed. The thorns dug into my hand as I looked around for the animal, I couldn't see much in the dark and had to feel around finding some fresh soil and an area by the bottom of the shed that had been dug recently, a small hole big enough for the time capsule, Ian had described it as a large metal money box with a hinged handle. The bastard dog had got to it and as I pulled my arm out I felt my arm brush against something warm and wet, I recoiled tearing my sleeve and cutting my arm on the thorns. I grabbed a stick and poked it back in, this time a human voice tried not to react as it struck them, it sounded female.

'Who's there?' I said.

There was a cracking noise from behind me, someone trying to creep up and a light shone into my face as I turned to see Horace with a flashlight at the corner of the shed. He was angry.

'Here, you want to find out then see for yourself.' I reached out to grab the light but the person in the bushes took the chance to get out, barging me to the floor running towards the fence where the garden perimeter met the woods. By the time I got up and reached it they were long gone and I scanned the woods with the beam counting trees and cursing my bad timing.

'It's too late now Davy, I told you to leave it alone.' Horace said.

'Why didn't you stop them, they must have pushed right past you?'

'They would still have taken it.'

'How?'

'The more you want it the more they're drawn to come and take it away from you. If not tonight then soon, somehow.'

He shook his head and began to walk back to the house.

'You could have just left, you had a last chance to get out Davy. The whole game has changed for you now.'

CHAPTER TWENTY-FIVE

Nineteen Eighty-Three, the last day of term at school and I was walking home with Charlotte, we'd stopped on a fallen tree in the woods and she had signed my shirt. I noticed there were kisses under the inscription too. I was quite happy because she'd split up with Carl, not for the first time but I was hoping it would be a chance for me to show her my feelings and he'd left school two years before which meant he wasn't hanging around so much. He'd also fallen out with some of the others at this point and when he got a moped he spent most of his time with Crazy Rick.

'Where are you going then?' Said Charlotte, handing me back my felt pen and nudging me playfully.

'I thought I was walking you home?'

'I mean after summer.'

'Oh right. I'm going to college if I get the grades.'

'Me too.'

'Where?'

'City College.'

'Really? Me too, we can get the train together.' I beamed at her and felt like things were turning a corner at last.

'I thought you were going to be a rock star?' She said.

'My parents have told me to get educated first and do it part time.

'I think that sounds best, they'll be loads of people at college.'

'I could play them the tapes we made in the garage, I can still form a band there.'

'It's a shame you stopped that band with Carl and the boys, I thought it was pretty good for what it's worth.'

'I'd just call it passable.'

She held my hand and turned it to see the scar, running

her finger along it.

'You written a song about me yet?' She lent into me and her hair brushed on my face.

I felt my cheeks burning, there had been endless poetry and attempts at songs but I couldn't tell her. When we stood up to leave she gave me a sweet smile and then she kissed me on the cheek, we walked through the back of the gardens into the Close and then we waited for her bus on the main road.

I was happy lost in a moment with Charlotte, talking about our future together at college. She was going away for the summer to her cousins and then coming back a week before the start of term. It was perfect, almost. It would have been if the bus had arrived on time.

There was a high-pitched motor sound getting louder, a moped approaching and as it came into view I saw that it was Carl.

I spotted him first and tried to move back on the bench in the wooden bus shelter so he wouldn't see us but he sounded his horn and saluted, double taking as he saw who I was with and turned into the Close a hundred yards further down the main road. The bus was late, I kept looking back down the road hoping for it to come so Charlotte could get on it and go home and we could then start our lives at college when we met again after the summer. Instead I heard the ominous sound of the moped coming back out of the Close. Carl bumped it on the pavement and pootled along to us. I nodded to him and he nodded back then he looked over at Charlotte who gave him a roll of her eyes and then stared back up the road.

'Alright Charlotte?' He said, taking his helmet off.

'Fine. I don't want to speak to you Carl.'

'I'm just being polite, we can still be friends.'

'You should go.' I said, 'We're waiting for the bus and having a private chat.'

'What about?'

'It wouldn't be private if we told you.' Charlotte said.

Carl gave me one of his looks, I remembered it well as his *'Watch this Davy'* look and I hated it.

'Charlotte, let me give you a lift home.'

'No thanks.' I said.

'Can't she speak for herself?'

Charlotte looked at me and then at him.

'Just a lift?'

'I'll go and get my spare helmet out the garage and you'll be home in no time.'

'But we're hanging out?' I said, wanting her to say no to tell him to piss off and leave us alone, I wanted to clout him one, it was his decision to break up with her and upset her again but he had a hold over her that I couldn't work out.

'Okay.' She said, twisting her mouth and folding her arms. 'You better be quick because if my bus comes I'm getting on it.'

Carl whizzed back to get the crash helmet and I sat there feeling angry with both of them, her for being so gullible and him for taking away the chance of a last goodbye before College. Charlotte didn't seem to be inter-ested in our chat anymore, she was busy checking herself in a small hand mirror from her pencil case as I prayed for her bus to appear.

It didn't and as they pulled away on the moped I could tell by the way she held onto his waist that it wasn't just a lift. She still loved him.

I walked back into the Close, past the empty plot of land and up our path. Inside I hardly noticed Mum and Dad whispering in hushed voices and waiting for me. My day was about to get worse, in fact my life was.

'Davy where have you been, we've been waiting for you.'

'I was walking Charlotte back from school.'

'Well sit down your father and me have got things to talk about with you.'

'Oh not this lecture again, I told you I'm going to go to college, I'll do the music part time just stop nagging me will you?'

I thought my dad was going to give me a telling off for being mouthy but I didn't care I was angry about what had just happened at the bus stop.

'Davy, as you've finished school now and you're going off to college we think it's time we had some changes too.'

'Changes?'

'I'm afraid that for a while now me and your dad have been thinking of what we want.'

'What you want?'

'We're separating Davy, just for a bit.' Said Dad.

I stared back at them wondering what they were going on about.

'It's just that when you have kids you sometimes drift apart and become more of a team and then sixteen years go by and you realise you want different things, we're sorry love but you can support us can't you?'

'Support you?'

'We still care for each other but we're not *in* love.'

I stood up.

'You're not separating, stop being so stupid, what's for tea?'

'Davy, we're sorry but it's going to happen.'

I got up and ran out the back into the garden and into the woods, up the trail to the road works. I went across the new road which now cut through the main trail, the second half of the woods now felt remote, separated by the horrible scar of tarmac. I turned east towards the farmland jumping the fence hardly breaking my stride and down the trail shrouded by trees that led to the train tunnel fence. I stopped for a few moments to catch my breath, holding the barbed wire with my foot and jumping over, tripping as I reached the embankment I fell, over and over on the rough limestone but I didn't care I *wanted* it to hurt I needed to fire off the adrenaline racing through my body, I yelled out as I came to a halt against some bushes, my face and hands bleeding.

I lay there for a while, staring up at the summer sky and wanting to disappear up into it and keep going forever and ever, away from the pain and hurt I was feeling.

I got up and went over to the side of the tunnel, lowering myself down on the tree roots and footholds. I stepped in front of the tunnel entrance and I yelled out at the top of my lungs like a wounded animal, I just let it go and screamed, running into the void along the gravel, sliding and stumbling but not caring.

I needed to find Kane, I wanted him to come and get me and so I waited on the track, waited for the light at the other end to turn to black as a train entered and then the small pin prick of light appear, signalling the engine was coming.

It wasn't long before it happened and I made my way to one of the cubbyholes, closing my eyes as the whining track echoed, the wind picked up as it neared I shut my eyes tighter because I knew any moment Kane would be there with Adam and I could at least go off with them and escape, maybe I could learn to stay there longer, even live there. It might have been a weird place but it was away from the pain I was trying to blot out.

The train whipped past and the metal on metal sound

of the wheels thundered through me, and then a quieting fade. I opened my eyes but there was nothing, just an empty tunnel, I looked left to see a tiny speck of light again at the far end of the tunnel then to the right to see the back of the rear engine as it went further away.

It seemed Kane had left me too.

* * *

I went back several times over the next few weeks, hoping that he would appear but there was no sign of him or Adam or even Bilbo. I was so desperate to see even that mangy old mutt appear but I was alone.

One evening I came back across the woods and saw signs and yellow lights across the new road, a large board was detailing the opening date and the Mayor would lead a procession and be the first to drive down it. Our woods looked and felt much smaller than they once had done, it took far less time to get home through the trail to the gardens. Once the road was open it would be a hazard to cross over, bringing a permanent divide between me and the world we had discovered and spent our childhood in.

The night before the road opening I sat in the park drinking Loz's Dad's home brew with him and the twins talking about what we were going to do next with our dreams, careers, life.

We climbed up onto the park keepers shed roof and watched the sun going down, giggling with the effects from the nasty sedimented ale.

I thought I was seeing things at first; Charlotte appeared from the woods running over to the swings. She was screaming, then I saw Carl behind her, he caught up with her and they fell to the ground, laughing and rolling around.

Loz stood up on the roof and shouted over to them.

'Dirty sods.'

They looked over and waved, the others got down and joined them over by the swings; I sat there finishing the ale even though it was by then hurting my stomach. Eventually they were calling over to me so I got down and walked over slowly.

'Hey Davy.' Said Charlotte.

'Hi.'

'You okay?'

'I thought you were going to your cousins for the summer?'

She looked at Carl who grinned at me smugly.

'I was but Carl and I are back together so I asked my Mum if I could stay here.'

'Great.' Said Peter.

'So we can still all hang out for the summer.' She said.

Carl reached in his pocket and got out some cigarettes.

'Except we're going camping for a week to the coast so it's not the whole summer.'

I decided that I had heard enough and began to walk off.

'Davy, where are you going?' Shouted Ian.

'I'm leaving.'

'But it's early.'

'Time for beddy byes?' Carl laughed.

I stormed back over and stood over him, shaking.

'I mean *I'm leaving here for good* you twat.'

Carl puffed on his cigarette and blew some up towards me. He always pretended to inhale the smoke but never did, he thought he looked hard though.

'Ha, that means you want to kiss him.' Said Ian.

'What?' Said Carl.

'Blowing smoke in his face.'

'Do you want a smack?' Said Carl.

'Hey.' Said Peter standing up from one of the swings. 'You touch my brother and you're dead.'

'Davy you can't leave, you start College in September.' Charlotte said.

'Well I won't be there. Everything round here is turning to shit, just look at it.'

'Oh I don't know, I like it here.' Carl said. He kissed Charlotte in front of me and looked up with a smug expression, pulling her close. Instead of being like an affectionate hug it looked more like he had her in a headlock.

'Carl, this isn't comfortable.' She said.

'Stop doing that.' I said.

Carl stopped, let her sit back and stood up, getting in my face.

'Say that again.'

'You heard me, leave her alone you don't even want her it's only because I wanted to go out with her.'

'Hey I'm not some boys' toy.' Charlotte said.

'Get lost Davy.' Said Carl.

'I'll go when I want to.' I said. The rotten beer was starting to whirl in my stomach mixing with adrenaline, I used to get nausea before an altercation and it wasn't nice. As I looked at Carl I had flashbacks to Adam and the accident, I felt the white scar in my hand and the hurt that I felt over Charlotte. This was supposed to be one of my best friends and he had made my life hell.

'She thinks you're weird.' He said. 'In fact we *all* do with your stupid crap about the gallows and ghosts.'

'Is that right?' I said, looking around at the worried faces.

'Don't listen to him' Said Peter.

I was shaking and split between running or taking Carl on. He was twice as big as me but I was ten times madder.

'One day Carl,' I said, slurring, 'I'm going to come back and kill you.'

'Really?'

'You'll pay for all the things you've done.' I said.

'Oh, is that after your balls drop or when you find someone big enough?' He grinned.

'You'll see you shitbag.'

'*Shitbag*, is that the best you can do?'

'I'm off.' I said.

Carl took a few paces after me as I walked away.

'I think *Adam* would have come up with something better.' He turned to the others to wait for applause but all he got was a horrified silence.

I ran back and took a swing at him but with the drink it must have looked pretty lousy and slow. Carl dodged to one side and punched me in the guts, I felt the grass beneath me begin to wobble and I puked all over Carl's trousers and shoes.

The others were grossed out and backed away except Peter who was trying to help me stand up and as soon as I was upright I head-butted Carl as hard as I could sending him back into Charlotte's lap and they both fell over the back of the bench.

It was twenty-five years before Carl got the next punch in beside his Ferrari.

CHAPTER TWENTY-SIX

We pulled up on the forecourt to the estate that led to Carl's house. The twins and Loz were with me. We had spoken for ages about the right thing to do since the crash and felt that it was a showdown we all still needed.

To our surprise Carl had contacted us first and invited us over clearing it with the guard who had also received a hefty payment and some signed CDs of *The Sleeping Gallows* for the gatehouse 'incident'. It didn't stop him giving us a stern warning as we waited for the barrier to be lifted at the entrance even after Loz had handed him a four pack of beer as a peace offering.

We drove up through the estate and I realised just how different Carl's life in music had been to mine, not that it had changed him it had merely changed his surroundings, he was still a shit from what we could make out, maybe I was wrong but the last time I'd seen him before I'd left the Close we'd come to blows so we had kind of picked up where we left off.

It was about four in the afternoon when we arrived at Carl's house. Peter rang the intercom beside a set of eight foot high white gates.

'He likes to keep people out then?' Said Ian.

'I think it's to protect people from Carl.' I said.

'Hey Davy you're not going to go off on one in there are you? I thought we were just going to try and resolve things peacefully.'

'Best behaviour, I swear.'

We drove up through a long driveway sculpted through neat gardens that curved towards a detached house; there were more windows in there than some of the Hotels I'd stayed at during my travels.

The double door of the house opened up and there in Bermuda shorts and a white vest stood Carl, looking pale and drawn.

'Welcome to the Palace.' He said, shaking hands with Peter and Ian. 'I hope everyone comes in peace, what's with the Imperial Guard?'

'Interesting you might ask but its Loz, remember the Cadets abseil weekend?' I said.

Loz elbowed me. 'Leave it Davy, not now.'
I walked up to him, last in the line; Carl put his hand on my shoulder.

'Davy I think I need to thank you.'

'Yeah?'

'I needed a wake up call to clean up and I'm really going to give it a go this time.'

I reserved judgement on that one as we went inside. The place was a mess, clothes, CDs, and food packets littered the rooms. He showed us through towards the games room which was inside a huge dome conservatory leading to a garden with an outdoor pool.

'Make yourself comfortable lads and help yourself to some drinks.'

'The maid must be on holiday.' I said to Loz as I stepped on a take away tin.

The twins immediately started to set up the balls on the pool table.

'Winner stays on.'

I walked over to a long unit where a jug of coffee stood on a percolator.

'No booze then Carl?' I said.

'Not anymore my friend, you have to try this stuff Louise got imported, it's the best coffee I've ever had, forget your high street café bars.'

Loz flopped down on the sofa and removed his trooper helmet.

'It really is you.' Carl said, sitting beside him and putting his arm around him. 'Good to see you mate.'

I wasn't falling for any of the mister nice guy act; I knew Carl was playing us off against each other.

'So you've been doing well then with the music?' I said, looking at a gold disc on the wall.

'Alright I suppose.' He sniffed.

There were so many things I wanted to say to him but I had to be in control, so I drank my coffee and I bided my time as we chatted and played pool. I would pick my moment carefully.

* * *

By early evening it was actually Carl who started to steer the conversation round to my return, asking about the Police inquiry. I was beating him at pool, it was probably to put me off my shot but I wondered how he'd found out and asked him whom he'd heard it from.

'I can't remember exactly, I think I was in the hospital in recovery and overheard it.'

'Interesting.' I said, potting my last ball. All I needed was to sink the black eight ball to beat him.

'And they let you go just like that? Nice of them to do that, I mean murder charges?'

'Not when you're innocent.' I said, clipping the ball at too sharp an angle, it rolled to a slow halt and Carl grinned.

'Ooh unlucky.'

He potted two balls leaving just the eight ball again then he stopped the shot he was about to play, looked at me and went to say something.

Before he could there was a bang against the conservatory doors. We turned to see a big dog scratching and trying to get in, pawing at the handle, it was dirty, covered in mud and it looked crazy. Bilbo.

I stood still, unable to move as I looked at it, wondering what the hell it was doing here. Carl started shouting. 'Bloody mutt.' He went over to the doors.

'Don't open them.' I said.

Carl ignored me, 'He keeps doing this I only hosed him down an hour ago.' I watched as Carl edged out of the door and pushed the dog away towards the outdoors pool, chasing it. He grabbed a hosepipe and sprayed the animal, it barked and jumped around trying to swallow the jet. The others were laughing and the dog certainly seemed to enjoy it but I didn't feel good at all.

'What's the matter Davy?' Loz said.

'Nothing, I thought it reminded me of Bilbo that's all.'

'Yeah, it does now you mention it, didn't he have a lame leg or something?'

Carl walked back into the house puffing and wiping mud from his jeans.

'Mad dog.'

'Davy was just saying he looks like Bilbo.'

'Ha, and you shit yourself?'

'Funny.' I said.

'I found him at the rescue centre a few years back and that's what I thought so I ended up coming home with him. Stupid really, I'd only gone to take a girlfriend there with a stray she'd picked up on the side of that road, the one up near the Close.'

'You still pass it? You should have knocked and popped in.' Said Loz.

'I sometimes do on the way into the City but I can't bring

myself to go into the actual Close, too many memories of the folks.'

'Do you avoid the Zoo as well?' I said.

He looked at me puzzled, Peter rolled his eyes, he knew where I was going with it.

'There is something I thought we need to discuss Carl, music wise.'

He nodded slowly then switched on a big smile for the others as he turned to them in the conservatory.

'Yeah, sure. Look sorry lads, I just need to clean up a bit first, bit of a date later but help yourself to anything you want.'

'Hey we haven't finished the game.' I said.'

'Oh I wouldn't have missed that ball Davy, come on.'

'Take the bloody shot then.'

He laughed and disappeared for a while and we carried on playing pool and talking about old times. I wondered if the guys had simply forgotten everything he'd done to us.

Loz was spending ages trying to have a crap in the downstairs toilet so I went in search of a toilet and found Carl at the top of the stairs staring at himself in a mirror; he'd changed into a fancy black shirt and trousers.

'Alright Davy?'

'Just wanted a piss but Loz is stuck in the other one.'

'Second right down that way.' He said, trotting downstairs, full of himself.

I called after him. 'We need to talk Carl.'

I wandered down one of the corridors and found another bathroom, took a leak, checked the medicine cabinets for any drugs he might be hiding. I couldn't help but snoop around the rooms, they were massive. I eventually came to the main bedroom and stifled my laughter at the leopard print bedcover.

I thought I'd spent long enough up there and before Carl got suspicious I made my way back to the stairs completely missing the picture of Charlotte on the window ledge among a cluster of frames.

In the games room the twins were laughing and joking about something with Carl. When I appeared they went quiet then Carl clapped his hands together and cleared his throat.

'Right you lot, as much as this has been a blast just one more game and then it's chucking out time, I have a guest coming to dinner.'

'Lady?' Loz said.

'A *very special* lady.'

'You wanted to chat about something Davy?' Carl said as we watched the twins begin the game.

'The song.'

'Which one.'

'The one we wrote together.'

'Hang on, you're losing me here?'

'The Sleeping Gallows?'

Ian missed his shot and looked over. Carl stared at me then the others, pointed his thumb and did an impression of Ricky Gervais in *Extras*.

'Is he havin a laff?'

'Carl, we've got a tape, from the garage sessions.'

'Sessions? You call them sessions? I call it Ian on a load of washing up boxes, Peter on the spoons, Loz on a triangle and you and me playing Beatles covers, badly!'

'We wrote our own stuff too and *The Sleeping Gallows* was one of my ideas, if anything I let you use it and develop the bridge. The chorus and verses were done already.'

Carl walked over so he was stood under his Gold disc as

if making a point.

'Davy, this is nonsense mate, we made a racket, that song was nothing to do with you.'

'Come on Carl, the name was from the Close.'

'Okay so I may have used the title but nobody owns the rights to a name like that.'

'So you deny us recording it?'

'Yeah.'

'So you can't remember?'

'I remember you had a tough time, and I know what happened to Adam was bad so I don't blame you but as I recall you went off the radar and we stood by you.'

'That's bullshit.'

'You created an invisible friend, what was his name?'

'Kane.' Said Loz walking out of the downstairs toilet, pieces of his outfit hanging off the elastic body suit underneath.

I glared at him. 'What?' He shrugged.

'Kane, that's it.' Carl smirked. 'So all that kind of eclipsed the lousy songs we may have bashed out in the garage.

'We have it on tape.' I said.

'Oh bravo, you really are clever Davy. He clapped his hands loudly. 'So you can supply my record company with a copy, we can try mediation before you take me to court and successfully sue my arse off?'

The room fell silent. I looked at him and realised that I had to bluff this, the capsule had been taken but he wasn't to know that. He walked over to the Twins.

'Now can we let the boys finish their game?' Carl said.

I walked over to him and got in his face.

'I often wonder what would have happened if Charlotte's bus had been on time that day.'

'Davy I'm in recovery having a nice time with my old friends here, why do you insist on dragging up all this dirt?'

'The day you turned up on that hair dryer of a motorbike and slimed your way back in.'

'Oh, this is about Charlotte now? I'm sorry she liked me but I hear she's single these days so why don't you get in there?'

'This isn't just about Charlotte it's about everything you took from me.'

Carl reached into his pocket and got out a wad of rolled up notes.

'If it's money you needed then why didn't you just ask?'

'Bloody hell.' Said Ian, 'There must be thousands there.'

I looked at the money and shook my head.

'You don't get it do you Carl?'

'Get what Davy, that you're still a head case who we have to put up with because we feel sorry for you? Grow up you miserable bastard we stood by you for years when others avoided you, even Rick said you were weird and *he* was a nut job.'

I pulled back my fist, he held his arms up but I simply tweaked his nose and made a honking noise.

'Got your nose!' I said, poking my thumb through my fingers. 'Come on lads, I'm bored and it's time we were leaving.'

Carl was red with rage, speechless for once.

'See you in court then I guess?' I pushed the front door open and made my exit.

On the way back out of the estate we were too busy talking about the time we'd just spent with Carl to notice a car going past us the other way. If we had we would have seen a familiar female on her way to the house to attend a dinner invitation and she came bearing a special gift.

CHAPTER TWENTY-SEVEN

My Dad stood at the end of the garden just as he had done years ago, I looked around for a ball to kick, I used to like that when I was younger, talking to Dad about stuff I'd done that day while we kicked the ball to each other and Adam would play too when he was there.

'Davy, I'm going back to Canada.'

'But we've not really had a chance to catch up.' I said.

'I know and I've been meaning to apologise to you son.'

'Apologise for what?'

He prodded a section of loose wood in the fence and tried to lock it back into place, an aversion technique he used when talking about sensitive stuff, I remember when Adam died he would always be doing something like fixing my bike or a kitchen drawer, he wouldn't look at me after the accident, it was like he blamed himself for how things turned out.

'When the Police contacted me in Canada and presented me with all the evidence I'm afraid I wasn't sure.'

'You believed that I killed someone?'

'No, but I wasn't bloody sure enough that you *didn't* and I feel so bad about that.'

'Hey Dad look don't blame yourself, you hadn't seen or heard from me for years so how would you know how I'd turned out.'

He seemed surprised by my reaction, deep down I was upset of course but he'd been through enough, we all had.

'You could come with me back to Canada if you want to. I spoke with the solicitor, he says the Police couldn't stop you unless they put you under house arrest here.'

'I might stay on just a bit more first. It's been good to catch up with the lads.'

'Including Carl?'

I shook my head.

'You still blame him for Adam's death don't you son?'

'Partly yes. I've relayed that accident over and over and wonder if I'd done this or that, if I'd found my own way back Adam never would have had to take me down that trail in the first place but it was Carl who I keep seeing as the wrong piece in the picture.'

'I've done the same thing Davy, it was me who told him to escort you but no matter how much we torture ourselves...'

'Nothing's ever going to bring Adam back is it?'

He put his hand on my shoulder and shook his head.

'He'd be a middle aged man now, imagine that? I still see him running around with Airfix kits and squabbling with you. I never got to do the stuff with either of you though, go to the pub, football matches, share the experiences of growing up into a man. Sometimes I feel like I lost both of you that day.

'Was Carl as bad as I recall when we were younger? I mean he's still a dickhead now but back then I used to give him the benefit of the doubt and just get on with being friends.'

'I don't know, I wasn't there when you were messing around, all I know is that the other parents had concerns over the years, I guess we saw that he liked trouble more than most and you guys followed him like the pied piper for years although none of you were angels.'

'Did you go to his parent's funeral?'

'What funeral?' Said Dad.

'After their mishap with the Elephants.'

'Davy what are you talking about?'

'Carl's parents and the thing with the Elephant?'

'They went on a world tour but they're not dead.'

'Mum told me they were killed.'

Dad shook his head. 'Are you sure?'

'Yeah. She must have told you?'

'My contact with your mum has been sporadic at best over the years but there's been some mistake because Carl's parents moved to Australia and last I heard they were in fine health, in fact Derek e-mailed me some pictures after looking me up on a networking site.'

'The twins and Loz remember it, I'm not making it up.'

'I don't know the answer, to be honest I find coming back here really difficult, I always had trouble thinking straight here ever since Adam died. I've never really spoken to anyone about it but it was part of why I drifted from your mum and eventually had to go away. I forgot huge chunks of memory when I left but now I'm back it's like...'

'Like something's over your shoulder?'

'Turn around and it's gone. I never figured it out.'

'Did you see things too?' I said.

He looked into the woods and took a deep breath.

'It stopped almost as soon as I got on the plane when I left but whenever I thought of this place I got a migraine, really bad and so I had therapy over in Canada, the guy did wonders for me, trance therapy.'

There was a rumble in the ground, at first I thought it was a train below then I looked up to see the sky was blackening in the distance, a storm was coming, a huge storm.

'Maybe. I could use a lay down before dinner.'

I had so many questions but just as I began to get to the heart of it Dad seemed to close down and not want to discuss it.

'Are you coming in?' Dad started to walk back to the house just as Horace appeared; he saw us and took off his trilby hat when he passed my dad who just ignored him as he did most of the time, it seemed to be the grown up thing to ignore the obstacles in life and get on with living.

'Do you have a minute Davy?' Said Horace.

'Sure.'

'Let's take a walk.'

My dad called out from the back door.

'Where are you off to?'

'Just be a few minutes.'

'Okay well don't be long, I'd like to sit together for a meal like the old days?'

I knew this meant that Horace wasn't invited. I waved and followed him into the woods and round into his garden, squeezing through the fence.

'You should get a gate put in here you know.' I said as I moved one of the slats out the way.

'Only attracts unwelcome visitors.' He said as I held it up for him to pass through. 'I thought you might want to know that your dad is right, you should go back with him to Canada, there's still time.'

'How do you know what we were talking about?'

'Your Mum mentioned it.'

'Oh.'

Horace paused by the side of the train tunnel chimney, a wind crept around us and the smell of metal and dust seeped out, a train was coming, I knew the sound even though I wasn't inside the tunnel.

'Davy some people you thought were close to you have been playing you as a fool. You can't run yet, you're way past that now so you need to work it all out.' He got his pipe out and began fiddling with it. 'Can you hear it?'

'What?' I said.

I could sense the ground move and another noise from the tunnel chimney.

'A second train?'

The wailing began to creep up out from below as the air was pushed up and out of the grills.

'See how unthreatening it is when you discover the truth?' Horace said.

I followed him round the tunnel chimney towards the old shed. He motioned with his pipe towards the hole in the ground.

'Think about it, the time capsule is a place to start, who knew it was there and what was the motive to take it?' He lit his pipe and blew a plume of smoke into the air, it rose up and mixed with the light rain that had begun to fall.

'You mean someone stole it to take to Carl? Ian was the only person who knew where it was buried but he wouldn't do anything like that besides it was a woman's voice.'

Horace raised his eyebrow.

'His wife didn't like you much did she and who else knew where it was, Peter, Loz?'

'But Ian wouldn't get involved with something like that. He hates Carl.'

'Does he? Don't ever make the mistake of thinking you really know anyone Davy. Not even yourself.'

Horace began to walk off down the garden towards the house, the rain grew heavier and I pulled up my shirt collar.

'Horace, where is this all leading?'

'Where all life leads Davy. No matter how many twists and turns, mysteries and adventures it's only heading to one thing ... death.'

CHAPTER TWENTY-EIGHT

I burst into Ian's house, surprising him. Liz and the kids were out at the shops.

'Davy, what the hell?'

'Where is it you cheating bastard?'

'What?'

'The tape, you were in on it stealing the tape before I could get to it.'

'No, you've got it wrong.'

I grabbed him and pushed him onto the stairs.

'Listen I'm not in the mood for games, where is the bloody time capsule?'

He was shaking.

'In the back shed.'

I walked through the hall into the kitchen, out the back and down to the shed at the bottom of the garden.

'Combination?' I shouted as Ian caught up with me.

He pushed in front of me and undid the lock. 'You've got this wrong Davy.'

'Have I?'

I walked into the shed and looked around, spotting a metal box on a shelf. There was a bang and I turned to see Ian had locked the shed behind me.

'Ian I'll kick this bloody door straight off its hinges so open up.'

'Not until you listen to me, please.'

'What is there to listen to. You double crossed me.'

'No I didn't.'

'It was a woman's voice that night, who did you get to do it, your wife?'

'No, please calm down and I'll explain everything.'

I held the box and tried the handle, knuckles white with

rage and my head against the door like Jack Nicholson when his wife locked him in the storage room in *The Shining*. I could feel my stomach turning and usually I was in danger of blacking out like that so I had to calm down and think straight. Ian was scared and deserved a chance to explain.

'Okay, let me out and let's talk like sensible adults.'

* * *

We sat in the middle of the trampoline, tipping the box contents out, bits of paper fell out with our names on them, poems, toys, painted eggshells that had smashed, a faded photograph of us in the Close, me with my red guardsman outfit and busby.

Ian explained to me what had happened. He had received a call from Carl asking him if he wanted his time capsule back. At first he didn't know how he had come across it or if he was bluffing but then he mentioned that all he wanted was the tape and the rest belonged to Ian. He offered to hand it over on the condition that he didn't tell me about it. If it had been Peter he might have out-snookered Carl but Ian was more of a pushover.

'Like I said, it's all he wanted and I couldn't do anything could I, he offered me some money to take the family on holiday. We haven't been for three years.'

'So Carl has the bloody tape that I need to prove we wrote that song together?'

'Why didn't you just take his money Davy there was thousands in that bundle he offered you. Who cares about a sodding tape?'

I pushed Ian backwards; he flopped over then bounced back like a jack in the box.

'You still don't get it do you? This isn't about the money

it's about proving that Carl is a lying shitbag with no sense of honour.'

'Can't you just move on Davy.'

'I thought I had done but he dug up the past and he knew what he was doing, he was sending up a huge V sign to wherever I was.'

'You think it was like a challenge?'

'Something like that, you know the funeral for his parent's was all bullshit?'

'What?'

'I don't know but my dad said they're alive and well in Australia.'

'I went to it. There were cars and caskets and corpses... hang on, no there wasn't, he said they had lost the bodies in the jungle and the caskets were empty... oh my God!' Ian fell back onto the trampoline again and shouted at the sky.

'Why is this happening to me?'

'Snap out of it Ian, you're fine.'

'Why couldn't I grow up in a normal road with normal kids?'

'They don't exist, everyone's a screw up one way or another they just hide it better than others mate. We're not part of some family in a cheesey cereal advert okay!'

He started putting the bits back in the box.

'I'm sorry your tape isn't still here Davy.'

'Okay look don't worry about that now, we need to figure out a way to get it back.'

* * *

We went inside and called Peter and Loz, explaining what had happened and at the same time I told them all about the fake funeral that at first shocked them into disbelief then it turned to anger. Liz came back from the shops and it didn't take long for her vinegar face to convince me to leave. I borrowed Ian's car and headed over to Charlottes and told her everything that had been happening. We sat there trying to figure out the pieces of the puzzle Carl had left across our lives.

In the background the news on the TV spouted out its usual gloom, a couple of squatters in the City had been found after a neighbour complained about the smell. The country was going to hell in a handbag and I wanted to get out, follow my dad to Canada and make a new start but I was about to find out Charlotte had something to add to the mix, she turned off the television, held my hand and stroked the top of it, kissing it softly. .

'Do you remember that day in the Bus shelter?' She said, 'Sometimes I used to wonder if Carl hadn't turned up that day if things had been different, I would have gone to my cousins, come back and gone to college with you. Instead I spent the summer with Carl and the others, worrying about whether you were safe and then Carl convinced me to go travelling, it cost my parents a lot of money that course, they couldn't get much money back. I would sometimes feel so bad that I cried but Carl used to say '*it's your life, take what you want*'. I was so smitten that I tried to believe it but it wasn't me.'

'He said you thought I was creepy.'

'No, oh no Davy, you were always so sweet and good but I never realised back then.'

Charlotte's eyes began to well up I put my arm around her and held her close, kissing the top of her head. She looked up at me and I felt her breath on my face, I moved closer still and she reached up with her lips to meet mine. She put her hand on my shoulder and pulled me tightly, I pushed my hands through her hair as I'd wanted to for so many years and it felt softer than I could ever have imagined.

She pulled away and laced her fingers through mine.

'Davy, make love to me.'

'Really?' I said, rocking back on the couch.

She nodded and took me by the hand to the stairs. We'd got halfway up when the doorbell rang.

'Bollocks.'

'Leave it.'

There was a banging and a repeated ring again, Charlotte marched over. 'Who the hell is it?'

'Police. We'd like to speak to Davy please.'

Charlotte opened the door.

'Sorry to bother you Miss.'

It was the same inspectors who had interviewed me in the cells. They walked in out of the rain and gave me a knowing grin.

'How did you find me here?'

'A tip off about a stolen car and they managed to identify the driver, just so happened we were looking for the same guy and here we are.'

'Bitch, she's always disliked me.'

'Who?'

'The woman who called you.'

'Davy, we're not really interested about the car, we've got some developments from Malaysia regarding the Lifeguard and thought that it was important you should know about them.'

'Go on.'

'The report from the autopsy confirmed that the guy drowned, alcohol levels indicate he was seven times over the limit.'

'So Chuck died from his own stupidity, how does that

affect me?'

'It means that you are clear on that one, its good news Davy, why do you look so worried?'

Charlotte squeezed my hand.

'You tracked me down to tell me that?'

'It doesn't mean we won't need a chat at some point about the other things.'

'Other things?'

'Your friend from the bar, he's showing signs of recovery, he will be able to fill us in on what exactly happened that night.'

'I told you, it won't be anything to do with me.'

'Well, we need to reserve judgement for now but besides that it's a messy world out there, only today we discovered a double murder in the City, two squatters were found. Have you been to the city lately Davy?'

I shook my head I wasn't going to give them anymore excuses to take me in for questioning.

'I'm not accusing you I was just pointing out what a dangerous place it is at times.'

They stood up and walked towards the door.

'Oh there was one thing Davy.'

'Yes?'

'My friend here, his colleagues have recovered a woman's body from the same river they found Drew in. It's going to take some time to identify her so it would help us if you kept local for a while.'

'You can't just come in here and play around like that, I know what you're doing.'

'What's that?'

'Mind games. I know that without house arrest I can go where I want to.'

'If you go to Canada with your father then it might save

us extraditing you, so knock yourself out.'

'How do you know about that?'

The English inspector opened the door and walked out, I followed the Canadian guy as he reached the doorstep and turned to face me.

'Five across still missing Davy. You worked it out yet?'

He backed away down the path and I noticed something, a small rag doll hanging out of his raincoat pocket on a piece of string.

CHAPTER TWENTY-NINE

I should have felt really angry and unhappy as I headed up the garden into the woods to meet the guys and discuss Carl, the Police were still trying to scare me, I didn't have the tape to prove the song was mine but I was grinning, holding my bag of off-license booze and whistling *The Sleeping Gallows*.

I turned east and walked through the woods, over the new road which was quite tricky at certain times of the day, reaching the other side towards the farmer's field. Everything looked brighter and much more rosy when you were in love and I realised that I had *always* been in love with Charlotte, she was the missing thing over my shoulder, the part that I was looking for but could never find, the reason I'd kept running because I never thought I could ever have her. Horace said we chose to forget some things but I'd remembered the most important piece of buried time before it was lost forever.

I arrived at the edge of the tunnel woods and saw a thin plume of smoke in-between some trees at the top of the path. The twins and Loz sat round a small fire cooking potatoes in foil and sausages on sticks.

'So, which one of you is Robin Hood?'

'I think Loz is Friar Tuck.'

The Storm Trooper mumbled and waved his white armoured hand about.

'Davy, I'm sorry about the car thing, I never reported it missing.' Ian said.

'Doesn't matter mate.'

'You sure?'

'Yeah, give us a potato or something I'm starving.'

'You're a bit chirpy aren't you?'

'Why shouldn't I be?'

'Oh my God someone's in love.'

'I have the right to be happy like anyone else.'

The lads looked at each other.

'Davy, we do have something to tell you about the tape.'

'Can't we just enjoy ourselves and forget about Carl and all that rubbish for a bit lads.' I threw a can over to Peter.

'We think you need to know.' He said.

'I don't actually care anymore, Carl can stick the tape up his arse I'm finally feeling good to be back home where I belong, I may be picking up where I should have started when I was sixteen but hey, second chances don't always come along.

'Davy, you have to listen to us, you're being set up.'

'What?'

'Tell him.' Said Ian.

'He doesn't want to know.'

'Alright, you bastards are determined to ruin my happy mood so give me your worst, I've had the Police trying to stir things up this week about a body in a river thousands of miles away so I don't think you're going to top that.'

'I went over to front Carl out.' Said Peter. 'The funeral stuff you told us about and a few things Ian told me about the tape and the time capsule.'

'Why didn't you wait for me?'

'I knew you two would wind each other up, I went to try and off foot him, as an old mate, see if he would gloat and sure enough, he told me loads.'

'Like...?'

'You said it was a female who took the tin?'

'Yeah.'

'It was Charlotte.'

'No way.'

'That's what he said. He still has a picture up in his room.'

'But he disowned their daughter.'

'Apparently that's all being sorted out.'

'We've just spent the most amazing two days together I think I would know, she hates the guy.'

'She's using you, according to Carl she's been having dinner with him and they've been seeing each other again.'

'Seeing?'

'Shagging.' Said Loz.

Peter threw a stick at him. 'Loz, shut up.'

'Sorry.'

I sat there staring at the dead eyes of his Storm Trooper mask, stumbling for things to say, my mind reeling and cross wiring, fusing so many thoughts together at once.

'Bollocks. It's Carl talking shit again. Can't you see?'

'Sorry mate. I think he's telling the truth this time.'

'Bastards.'

'Hey Davy, we were trying to help.'

I took off with a half bottle of whisky, marching across the back of the farmers lane down to the tunnel woods. I slid down the embankment to the tunnel banging against the tree roots and limestone, the whisky bottle smashing in my pocket and cutting into me but I didn't care, I could feel myself blacking out and I had to keep moving, I had to get to the tunnel.

I waited for ages in the cubbyhole, bashing my fists on the cold wall until they bled. I was about to give up when I saw a train coming into the tunnel at the other end. To my right I could see another train coming down the other track, two of them, that was it, two passing trains.

I shut my eyes; all I could see was Carl and Charlotte, laughing at me, why had she been so two-faced and willing to be party to this? It physically hurt when I thought about it and the wailing noise and thundering trains were a welcome relief.

This time when I opened my eyes the train was there but no sign of Kane, Adam or Bilbo. The door swung open on it's own and I walked along the carriage and boarded it myself as it began to rumble back along the track. I waited as it clacked and swayed along the tunnel and out to the old platform which was covered in the thickest fog I had ever seen.

The trail that was usually littered with travellers and soldiers was empty, just that low thick fog and the sound of distant thunder.

I arrived at the courtyard, it was deserted and my vision was limited by the fog as I passed across past the well and turned to go into the alleyway. I could barely make out my own steps. I felt a breeze on my neck and turned, a small shadow darted back into the fog and a bird flew overhead.

I continued faster towards the end of the alleyway where I could just about make out the gallows, the sound of a drum echoed as it beat out a Celtic rhythm. Perched on top of the gallows was the bird that had flown past me, I could see now that it was a hawk. Below, on the platform was a hooded figure, a noose around the neck. The hawk flew down onto the old wooden cart. I noticed a piece of paper nailed to it and made my way over. I could see my name in italic inky writing. I pulled it away partly tearing it, untied the thin red string and prized the wax seal opening the note.

Five Still Missing

From out of the mist I could see a figure, it was Kane in his long coat trudging through the muddy yard.

'Worked it all out yet?' He said.

'No.'

'I think our reunion is coming to an end, you're closer than you think.'

'What does it mean?' I held up the piece of paper.

'You'll find out soon enough.'

'Okay can't you skip the cryptic clues and just tell me?'

Kane laughed.

'What's so funny?' I said, sitting down on the platform. Kane walked up the steps on the other side. He prodded the figure, adjusted the noose and tightened it under the neck.

'My head is going to explode if I don't get some answers soon.'

'You thought Charlotte was in love, that things were starting to work out at last?'

'I was so close to being okay, being normal and getting a happy ending, why is that so difficult? Everyone else does it.'

'They're just better actors than you, sure they look happy but behind closed doors it's very different.'

'I don't believe you, there's got to be something out there that's better.'

'So you're going to let Carl have the last laugh again eh? He gets the girl, he takes the song.'

'No, I just don't know how to play this out yet.'

'You need to work quickly, the Police aren't stupid you know.'

'They haven't got anything on me, it's all bullshit.'

'Is it?'

'You know it is.'

Kane walked back and forth behind me, his boots tapping

along the platform in the rhythm of the drum. It started to rain the drops got faster and heavier, the thunder crackled above us and I looked up into the slate sky, it was like an electric storm.

Kane grabbed the rope and pulled at it.

'Want to see Adam?'

'That's not him is it?' I said, panicking.

'No. He's over there.'

I looked across to where Kane was pointing and out of the fog came my brother, bent over and twisted like the day I'd seen him fall out of the coffin at the Churchyard, a toy drum strung over his neck beating it in time like a deformed clockwork toy.

Bilbo hobbled behind, the lame mutt with its manky coat and dribbling mouth.

'Where were they hiding?' I said.

'They weren't hiding.' Said Kane, bending down and sitting beside me. 'They're all in here.'

He tapped my head hard with his knuckles.

'Ouch.'

'You putting the pieces together yet?'

'No, I think you're as mad as I am.'

'I'll help as much as I can but you need to start remembering how we did it last time.' Said Kane.

'How *we* did what?'

'Can you remember where the accident happened?'

'Of course'

'It's where the new road crosses the old trail.'

'So what?'

'You need to go there tonight at nine as dusk falls and take Charlotte.'

'Why?'

'Think Davy, think how far you've travelled and what

you've done, all those countries, all those... 'incidents', The Nightclub Bouncer in France, Drew and Lucinda, Chuck, oh and the squatters, they were a surprise for me to deal with.'

'For you to deal with?'

'Who do you think tidies up your mess when you decide to take out your rage on people like Petra and Mr Dreads?'

'But you weren't with me, you were here, you stayed *here*.'

'No Davy, I was there, at every bloody sickening moment to pick up the pieces and prop you up while you go off on one of your little episodes.'

I began to feel sick, images flashing through my head, the picture of Drew the Police showed me, the one of the Lobster faced tourist in Spain, Petra in the squat and her dirty boyfriend grinning at me, trying to get me involved in their twisted lives.

'Shut up, you're not real, none of this is real.'

'You have one more thing to do. Can't you see the tables have turned to your advantage?'

'I don't want to hear anymore.'

'You *do* because it's why you came back, it's what you wanted to do since he caused Adam's death, you wanted revenge.'

'Shut up.'

'*Five is still missing*, you'll work it out now you're getting closer, go and see for yourself, let the scales fall away and then you'll know I'm right and what to do at nine tonight.' Kane pulled the bag off the head of the figure at the gallows. It was Carl. He looked straight ahead with his eyes wide but he couldn't see us, it was like he was trapped inside his own world.

Kane moved towards the platform mechanism and removed an iron guard-rail. The drum beat faster as

Adam bobbled around.

'Shit, get him down, I didn't want this.'

'Oh come now Davy, you do.'

'Please, don't.'

'Then save him.'

I got up and went over as fast as I could to Carl, Kane threw back the lever and the wooden hatch fell down into the platform, the noose creaked as the body followed and I lunged to try and support it. I had barely touched the swinging legs when Kane gave me a kick from behind and I fell into the open hatch down into the mud underneath the Gallows. It was dark and cold with little light coming through the open hatch and the ground was like wet clay in places. I reached around and grabbed a loose piece of wood. It snapped off and as I looked at it I realised it was a bone. I screamed out and a voice yelled at me.

'Keep the noise down, some of us are trying to sleep here.'

I turned to see Drew, his face rotting away, teeth protruding through his cheek as the flesh flapped about. I lost my breath and pushed my feet down so I could get away to the other end of the platform. Up popped Chuck, bloated and blue, he spat out a jet of muddy putrid water.

'No swimming today, can't you see the flags?'

I crouched up and went to my left, a hand reached out slapping me across the face, it was Petra, her hair matted and bloodied, lips bright red.

'Hey dirty boy, you decided to stay?'

Carl's feet had been swinging above us, now his body was cut loose by Kane and came down on me, throwing me back into the underside of the platform. I tried to loosen the rope from his neck.

'I'm sorry Carl, I'll get you out.'

His eyes popped open.

'Beat you Davy. I was dead first... too slow!'

I felt a scratch on my back; Bilbo was pawing through a gap in the wood, tearing at my shirt and growling.

Carl started to sing part of *The Sleeping Gallows*.

'*Nine o'clock,*
Trail of death,
The Sleeping Gallows...
Takes his breath.'

I pushed Carl away and moved to the back of the platform kicking out a panel, a hand grabbed my foot and before I could get out a rope was tightened round it and yanked me out like a rag doll round and round the yard by Kane on his horse. He was laughing and singing as Adam tried to catch me each time I went round, still beating his toy drum. Bilbo hobbled after him falling over and barking so loud that I couldn't think but I knew I had to free myself. The barking got higher pitched, louder until it was a wailing cry and then came a flash of lightning which hit the ground so close to me that I was thrown up into the air.

I opened my eyes and was back in the tunnel on the floor beside the cubbyhole as a train exited. There was blood where I had cracked my head on the gravel. I got to my feet; my face covered in blood, I had to get back to the Close quick, I had to see Horace and tell him what had happened.

CHAPTER THIRTY

I ran back through the farmer's field, over the fence, stumbling across the new road and nearly getting hit by a car. I went back down the trail to the houses and as I reached the gardens I veered towards Horace's, pulling the loose planks of wood away and slipping through into the garden round past the tunnel chimney The long grass had sprouted up overnight and I struggled to push my way through the overgrowth. Then, as I reached the other side of the chimney I stopped dead. The house was gone, the mown lawn, the plants, everything, all that was there was a derelict overgrown plot with a tall fence around it like it had been when I was a kid.

I collapsed onto my knees and tried to catch my breath and take it all in. I didn't know if I should laugh or cry, Horace had been my link between worlds. Kane spoke in riddles.

I got up and back out into the woods, round into mum's garden and into the house. She was at the kitchen table with the twins and Loz.

'Where's Horace?'

'Who?'

'The old neighbour, you're fancy man.'

'What neighbour, Oliver's family?' Said Loz.

'No, the guy with the Crossley.'

'Davy you're bleeding, sit down.' Mum stood up and rushed to the sink, wetting a tea towel and trying to dab it onto my head.

'Mum where is he?' I felt sick.

'You've had a bump dear, sit down I'll call an Ambulance.'

'Number Five, where is it?'

She looked at the others who shrugged.

'There's never been a number five Davy, are you feeling okay?'

That's when it hit me, *Five Still Missing*. Something or someone had been trying to tell me since I'd got back. I felt a nausea like my stomach was being scooped out, a sudden sharpness in my head and then spewed up over the table, it splashed across onto Loz then I collapsed.

* * *

When I woke up I was laid out on my old bed there was a paramedic in a green outfit looking down at me.

'Can you see me clearly?'

I nodded and tried to sit up.

'Gently as you go, you'll be happy to know it wasn't as bad as it looked, just a few stitches.'

My hand brushed the wire he'd just sewn into my head. He said something into his radio and then closed up his box of tricks handing me a glass of water.

'Take some of this.'

Charlotte appeared, the paramedic excused himself and went downstairs.

'You're okay then?' She said, leaning down to kiss me and I moved away.

'Do you care?'

'What's up?'

'Nothing.' I didn't want to let on that I knew she was betraying me.

'I'm just a bit shaken up, where are the others?'

'Downstairs, do you want to see them?'

'What do they know?'

'About what? I think Loz knows that sick wipes off his white armour easily.'

I looked out the window, it was getting dark, the Ambulance lights were flashing, a light drizzling rain forming a reflective haze across the Close.

'What time is it? I said.

'Nearly quarter to nine.'

'You have to come with me.'

'Where?'

'To the place where Adam died I have to show you something.'

She put her arm around me. I wished it hadn't felt so comforting I couldn't be with her after what she had been doing.

'You really did get a knock on the head, shall I get the chap back to look at you?'

'Charlotte, please, we have to go back there so I can find out the answer, he told me to be there.'

'Who?'

I could hear sirens in the distance, I knew the difference between ambulance and police cars, and time was running out.

'Come on, I'll explain on the way.'

I heard a knock at the front door, I looked out the window to see two police cars in the Close outside the vacant plot of land, where Horace's house had stood since I'd got back, until now. The two inspector's who had turned up at Charlottes got out and I knew time was ticking away fast for me.

I grabbed Charlotte by the hand. 'Just trust me.'

We walked quietly across the landing into Adam's room, out of the window and out onto the extension roof, from there I climbed down onto the top of the old coal bunker, Charlotte followed and slipped down with me holding onto her, she went to kiss me again but I pulled away, she'd betrayed me but I knew that there would be answers soon, answers to everything.

We walked behind the shed and were able to sidle along the fence to the garden gate and into the woods unnoticed. So I thought.

We ran into the woods and headed up the trail through the withering bluebells towards the new road crossing, towards the scene of the accident. The trail was muddy and a few times we stumbled and Charlotte stopped to catch her breath.

'What time is it now?'

'Ten to nine.' She puffed, 'Are you going to tell me where we're going?'

I slowed down as we came up towards the new road where it cut across the original trail, my heart pounding the blood around my body so fast that I could feel it in my ears like the beating of Adam's toy drum, tap, tap, tap. The rain was thin and cut across the moonlight in huge sheets like a graphic novel.

I looked around at the spot where the accident had happened across the road, I couldn't see anybody there. A few cars passed at speed, the limit along the road was supposed to be forty miles per hour but often they would speed up to double that in some parts. We walked over towards the trail on the other side, the wall of trees standing there like giant soldiers down the quarter mile or so of that stretch. I span around, looking up and down the road for signs of Kane, Adam, Bilbo, someone or something was going to show up.

'So what are we doing here?' Charlotte said.

'Waiting.'

'What for?'

'Nine o'clock.'

'What's going to happen then, the news headlines?' She laughed nervously.

I wiped away some of the rain from my face and spotted the tree, the place where it had all started, mum had put fresh flowers down recently and I picked them up and smelt them.

'I suppose in a way yes, news.'

'This is it isn't it, where Adam died?'

I nodded and placed the flowers back down, running my finger across the place where the chunk of bark was missing.

'Should have brought an umbrella, look at my hair.' She said.

'You look great, you always will do and that's my weakness.'

'Thanks.' She went to kiss me again as I stood up and I pulled away.

'What's wrong, why won't you let me kiss you?'

Before I could answer I saw a white flash across the road in the trees, a torchlight.

'Down.' I said, backing behind the tree. The light flickered around and came to rest near us. The person holding it came into view on the other side of the road. A shiny white glow from the moonlight gave his identity away. It was Loz, followed by the twins emerging from the other side.

'Davy, are you out here?'

They stood across the road waiting for a gap in the passing traffic, my little gang. I remembered the time I'd left, the day I'd walked up that new road when it opened, the guys had come to say goodbye to me, the Mayor's cartage and following vehicles honking their horns as they passed, the first vehicles to use it. I'd watched them all pass me by and kept walking past the junction, I'd got on the hard shoulder of the bigger main road and began hitching my way down to the coast, to the ferry that would take me away to a new start. I'd never planned to return.

It was five to nine I could hear sirens wailing, not just one this time there was many.

'Davy, what the hells going on?' Peter said, crossing the road to us.

'We'll find out soon.'

'Davy you've had a bang on the head let's go back mate.'

'Back to the Police? They know.'

'Know what?'

'What I did.'

'You said all those accusations were false.' Peter said.

I turned to Charlotte.

'I really loved and trusted you and you betrayed me.'

She looked confused.'

'Davy, the Police aren't after you,' said Ian, 'they wanted to track Carl down.'

'I don't believe you.'

'That song, the number one, he stole it off a couple of lads that had sent him a demo.

'But I helped write that song.'

'It might have been similar but it wasn't that one, the tape was unplayable at first but he had it restored and played it to Peter. There's nothing on it that sounds remotely like *The Sleeping Gallows*.

'That's not exactly murder!' I screamed over the rising noise. 'Why would they come after him for that, you're all in on this, it's a trap?'

From the woods on the other side of the road I saw the two Police Inspectors.

'Why are they here for me then?'

'The band tried to sue Carl so he attempted to get them killed but Louise found out and went to the Police.'

'So why are they here for me? You're lying.'

'There was another person he wanted them to kill.'
'Who?'
'He handed the 'hit man' a picture of you too.'
'Carl wants me dead?'
'You need to stick with us, it'll be okay Davy.'

I could now see Police lights in the distance, I turned and began to run towards the trail into the woods until I worked out what would happen next, I was confused as to why Kane would lead me to the Police like that or even into the path of Carl, I just needed to get some space, get back to the tunnel.

As I entered the woods I headed up the trail to the east towards the farmers field, I noticed a car thundering along from the opposite direction to the Police, heading towards them, headlights flickering. It was an old car, one I'd seen before, a gold coloured Crossley.

Inside there was a glow, the windows fogged and the driver was veering dangerously across both lanes. Horace.

From my vantage point up the trail I could see that the Police were getting closer to where the trail crossed the main road and behind the first squad car was a red Ferrari. Ian was right, they were after Carl, they were giving chase and he was heading straight towards Horace's car that was doddering around the middle of the road. I could see the Police were trying to stop Carl, they were nudging him towards the grass verge but they hadn't seen Charlotte and the others in the drizzling rain.

CHAPTER THIRTY-ONE

I ran back down the trail as fast as I could, racing towards the others, yelling for them to get out of the way. I reached the edge of the woods as Carl pushed the front police car out of the way, accelerating and at first looking like he was going to break for it but Horace's car was in the way, Carl hit the front corner of the Crossley and span off the road, onto the verge towards the group, towards Charlotte who was running in my direction for cover.

I dived pushing Charlotte out the way; the side of the Ferrari smashed into me throwing me into the edge of the woods. There was a crunching sound, sirens and shouting, I landed hard but bushes and a moss rotted tree stump softened my fall. I managed to roll over and kneel up, a stabbing pain in my side, a few ribs had probably broken but I could get up.

A Policeman had already tried to get Carl out of the car but it was wedged between two trees at an angle, like a compactor, one of them was the tree where the original accident had happened decades before. The Policeman had turned the engine off and they were now waiting for the fire brigade.

I staggered over to the Ferrari with Carl inside, his head bloodied, he was making a whining noise as his leg had shattered and he had internal bleeding from the impact.

The whole area stank of petrol that was pissing out of the back of the car onto the muddy verge. The Police were shouting at me to get back and wait for the fire engine but I ignored them.

He looked up slowly, trying to focus on me.

'I can't feel my leg.'

I lent on the side of the shattered window.

'Car too powerful for you was it?' I said.

'Help me.'

'Help you? Why don't you ask Charlotte.'

'Huh?'

'The tape, secret dinners, whatever else you two have been up to.'

Carl laughed and a line of spittled blood came out of his mouth, resting back on his chin.

'You are such a dickhead.'

'You're lying, I know she's been visiting you.'

'Piss off Davy.'

'You got her to steal the tape.'

He shook his head. 'Louise.'

'But Charlotte *did* visit you and there were pictures. Peter saw them and you told him you two were together.'

'I lied. I knew he'd talk to you okay? She just wanted to sort out some maintenance for our daughter I swear. Help me get out of this and we can straighten it all out.'

I looked at the door it was wedged shut there was no way he was getting out. I looked over towards the others and noticed Horace; he'd stopped his car and was walking towards us through the rain, playing with his pipe, packing tobacco into the top.

Carl spotted my scar.

'I certainly left my mark eh?'

'You did.'

'Must be why you play the guitar so shit.' He said, wincing.

I looked at it, the line across my palm, then at Carl, remembering the things he'd done, the way he'd manipulated all of us at some point. I turned and by the tree was Adam, sloping shoulder and bent in the moonlight, playing his little toy drum.

Kane was behind him, watching us, a building sound of

wailing began to fill the air as two trains passed underneath one of the tunnel chimneys.

The ground rumbled and the car dashboard lit up, the stereo came on, sounds of *'The Sleeping Gallows'* came out of the speakers.

'Hey, they're playing our song.' I said.

'My song.' Carl muttered through his bloody mouth.

I grabbed a crumpled pack of cigarettes on the edge of the dashboard and got one out, placing it carefully into his bloodied mouth.

'Sorry it's not a cigar.'

'What are you doing? For God's sake Davy the fire brigade will be here soon, I still have a chance.'

'You wanted to kill me.'

'Before you got to me. I knew why you'd really come back I remember what you said in the park when you left.'

'You had to try and hire someone, couldn't you do it yourself?'

Carl coughed up a jet of blood.

'Help me.'

'Like he helped your brother?' Kane shouted over the beating of the drum.

'It was an accident, I hated myself for it for years.'

'Why didn't you show it then?' I said.

'Davy we were kids.'

'Taking Charlotte away? That was no accident.'

'She wanted *me*, I can't help that.'

'The day you turned up at that bus stop we were about to start our new lives and maybe get together, you took that away from me.'

'She didn't like you in that way.'

'No?'

He began to laugh.

'What's funny?'

'She always thought you were weird, it was pity she felt.'

'You're just saying that.'

'Ask her.' He shouted.

I looked over at her, she was staring back at me, crying, traumatised. We had so much to talk about, there were many things that she might not understand but we had time, surely we had a chance? Horace appeared at the other side of the car, the rain thudding on the metalwork.

'So you turn up now. What happened to your bloody house?' I said.

'Number five is always missing. Nobody can ever build on the site of the gallows.'

Carl looked at me and then to the other side of the car.

'Who are you talking to?'

Horace lit his Pipe, leant in and pressed the cigarette lighter on the dashboard.

'I suggest you run Davy.'

'What are you doing?' Carl said, looking between me and Horace.

'Did I do those things Kane showed me? I have to know.'

Horace looked over at Kane, he was stood by Adam as he beat his drum and circled the trees and the car. They seemed to acknowledge each other and then he walked away, casually back towards his Crossley in the darkness, plumes of smoke rising up above his hat like a small steam engine going into a tunnel. I had a flashback to the day I'd first seen him at mum's house. I thought she'd seen him too.

'Don't leave me here.' Carl gripped my arm and I struggled to break free.

'Sorry. Got to go!' I turned to go but something snagged my shirt, I turned to see Carl, holding onto it with his bloody mitts, I tried to get him off, laughing nervously, I could see beyond the car that Horace was some way away near the road, he turned in the headlight beam of the Crossley and flicked open his Zippo lighter, the flame rising.

Adam beat the drum faster and faster, the sound got louder as I struggled to break free.

'Carl, you're always pulling me back.' I said, tugging as hard as I could but it was no use, his fingers were like iron nails in wood.

'Shouldn't be so slow.' He said.

'Get off.'

The sound of the song on the stereo filled my ears. Kane sang along and clapped in time to the drum;

> *'Nine o'clock,*
> *Trail of death...'*

'Carl let go.' I yelled out.

'Come on Davy, you know the song, we wrote it right?'

'You admit it?'

He nodded and started singing;

> *'...The Sleeping Gallows,*
> *Takes his breath.'*

Carl began to laugh and choke, thicker blood now coming out of his mouth, his eyes fogging over and rolling up into his skull. I saw Horace toss the brass Zippo towards the car, it arced up into the air and then back down.

'Better than being crushed by an Elephant right?' Carl whispered, his eyelids heavy, almost closed.

The cigarette lighter in the car clicked shooting out into his lap. He let go of my shirt as the Ferrari exploded into a fireball.

EPILOGUE

Carl's body ended up on top of the tunnel chimney in the missing number five plot in the Close, embedded onto the top grill like a well-done piece of meat at a barbeque. They didn't find him for weeks and when they did the corpse was in a sorry state, a nest of hawks had been using him to feed their young.

Charlotte got a lump sum through Carl's estate after proving he had been the father to their daughter and went on to marry Loz who got married in his Star Wars outfit. They decided to have a theme wedding. The Twins were the best men at the service and went as Luke Skywalker and Han Solo.

My body was never recovered although one of my shoes was found years later. A lad named Oliver from Gallows Close had been exploring the tunnel when it was thrown at him. Days later he returned to investigate further with some friends and discovered a cubbyhole. In limestone chalk writing he read;

Five Still Missing

Oliver was distracted by a whining on the tracks. A train was coming. He got inside the cubbyhole and as the train carriage stopped he looked up and saw me. I waved at him and pointed to the door as it swung open.

THE END ?

Lightning Source UK Ltd.
Milton Keynes UK
02 October 2010

160667UK00001B/7/P